I0651095

Richard Savage

**My Official Wife -  a Novel**

Richard Savage

**My Official Wife -  a Novel**

ISBN/EAN: 9783337023478

Printed in Europe, USA, Canada, Australia, Japan

Cover: Foto ©Andreas Hilbeck / pixelio.de

More available books at **www.hansebooks.com**

# COLLECTION

## OF

# BRITISH AUTHORS

## TAUCHNITZ EDITION.

VOL. 2771.

MY OFFICIAL WIFE. BY Col. R. H. SAVAGE.

IN ONE VOLUME.

.TAUCHNITZ EDITION.

By the same Author,

THE LITTLE LADY OF LAGUNITAS (WITH PORTRAIT) . . 2 vols.

PRINCE SCHAMYL'S WOOING . . . . . . . . 1 vol.

THE MASKED VENUS . , . . . . . . . . . 2 vols.

DELILAH OF HARLEM . . . . . . . . . . 2 vols.

THE ANARCHIST . . . . . . . . . . . . 2 vols.

A DAUGHTER OF JUDAS . . . . . . . . . 1 vol.

IN THE OLD CHATEAU . . : . . . . . . . 1 vol.

MISS DEVEREUX OF THE MARIQUITA . . . . . . 2 vols.

CHECKED THROUGH . . . . . . . . . . . 2 vols.

A MODERN CORSAIR . . . . . . . . . . 2 vols.

IN THE SWIM . . . . . . . . . . . . 2 vols.

THE WHITE LADY OF KHAMINAVATKA . . . . . 2 vols.

IN THE HOUSE OF HIS FRIENDS . . . . . . . 2 vols.

THE MYSTERY OF A SHIPYARD . . . . . . . 2 vols.

A MONTE CHRISTO IN KHAKI . . . . . . . . 1 vol.

# MY OFFICIAL WIFE

A NOVEL

BY

Col. RICHARD HENRY SAVAGE.

LEIPZIG

BERNHARD TAUCHNITZ

1891.

# CONTENTS.

## BOOK I.

### THE OFFICIAL WEDDING.

| | | | Page |
|---|---|---|---|
| CHAPTER | I. | The Bride. | 7 |
| — | II. | "What would Dick Gaines say to this?" | 22 |
| — | III. | Miss Vanderbilt-Astor. | 36 |
| — | IV. | Baron Friedrich. | 48 |
| — | V. | La Belle Américaine | 64 |
| — | VI. | My Wedding Dinner | 87 |

## BOOK II.

### A HORRIBLE HONEYMOON.

| | | | |
|---|---|---|---|
| CHAPTER | VII. | Opening Joys | 98 |
| — | VIII. | I Lunch with Baron Friedrich | 118 |
| — | IX. | Society Fêtes the Bride | 135 |

Page

CHAPTER     X.   Naughty Sacha. . . . . . . 155

—     XI.   The Pocket in the Ball-Dress . . 177

—     XII.   The Ignatief Ball . . . . . . . 193

## BOOK III.

### DISSOLVING THE BONDS.

CHAPTER XIII.   The Massage of Hate. . . . . . 210

—     XIV.   The Rat-Trap Closes. . . . . 220

—     XV.   Which Brother? . . . . . . 232

—     XVI.   The Last Coup of the Despairing

Rat   . . . . . . . . . 254

—     XVII.   At the Opera in Paris . . . . 272

# MY OFFICIAL WIFE.

## BOOK I.

### THE OFFICIAL WEDDING.

#### CHAPTER I.

##### THE BRIDE.

WE all shivered in the chilly winter air as the clicking wheels sped along over the plains of Eastern Prussia. Our fast express was approaching grim old Königsberg. Farm and village, wood and brook, marsh and river, flew by in a sort of wild dance.

Wrapped in rugs, snugly ensconced in the well-padded little compartments, our polyglot passengers dozed, smoked, grumbled, or chatted freely, as the varying spirits of the motley assemblage dictated. I had seen few of my *camarades de voyage,* as the cross-divisions of the little cars prevent in Germany our American excursions of discovery through the train.

The unusual hour of midnight is selected for despatching the "Schnellzug" from Berlin for St. Petersburg. In this I had realized the haughty scorn of the German railroad bureaucracy for popular comfort.

Bustling to the Friedrichstrasse station, the half hour before departure had given me only time to telegraph my friends at the Russian capital of my leaving Berlin, and to secure a through billet *via* Eydtkuhnen to the new Paris on the banks of the Neva. However, a night in a luxurious first-class carriage was no hardship to an old campaigner.

My preparations for the invasion of Russia were a good rug, a bunch of the least atrocious of various nicotian horrors on sale, some Tauchnitz volumes, and a few French romances as a sauce piquante to the rest. A capacious "Sinners' Friend" was filled and carefully tucked in the pocket of my warm Irish frieze ulster. It was mid-October, and in the moonlight the thin, stony fields looked starved, dug, and frozen out of all life. My immediate travelling companions were two handsome, stalwart, white-handed, jewelled-fingered Russian officers, returning to their native land after visiting entrancing Paris, so beloved by the Russ on his vacation.

Making my semi-bivouac upon the wide, soft seat on my side of the compartment, I soon dropped into slumber, leaving my military neighbors dallying lazily with the twisting of the little paper-tubed cigarettes, chatting about "shop," the girls they left behind them, and commenting on national matters with the daring freedom Russians love to affect abroad—a luxury denied them at home under the iron rule of the "White Czar."

As morning dawned, the old walls of Königsberg (the crowning place of the Prussian kings) opened to us. Through fosse and ditch we threaded heavily armed outworks, winding slowly into the heart of the last principal city of warlike Prussia near the Muscovite border.

After breakfast my military companions again betook themselves to the enjoyment of "baccarat," and the perpetual sacred fire of the papyrus. From their conversation I discovered them to be Captain Gregory Shevitch and Lieutenant Alexis Michaelovitch of the "cream of the service," the Russian Imperial Guard.

In the characteristically good French of their nation they discussed current topics, as the varying card battle decided the ultimate disposition of any pocket money not permanently invested in Paris.

Conning my book, comforted by a cigar, their conversation had great interest for an American ex-army officer, visiting for the first time their romantic land. My ears were open as I listlessly turned the wearying pages. They canvassed the recent appointment of a redoubtable ogre of official malignity as chief of the Russian Secret Police.

This gentleman, though of German not of Slavic descent, had powers unparalleled, even for a despotic land. From his concealed eyrie at St. Petersburg this Machiavelli struck by invisible hand everywhere. His high rank, plenary authority, and grave functions gave him untrammelled access to the new czar; all his lightning strokes were in that august name.

"Gregory," said Alexis, "I am told that the Nihilists are very active now, and working with energy to reopen their mail and telegraph communications, which Loris Melikoff cut off."

"That's so," replied Gregory (as he gazed on his cards with the money-grabbing instinct of a cunning Slav), "those poor devils can't get over our frontiers without a close shave on Siberia for life, or—something worse. The new head of the police has the sagacity of a Bismarck and the cunning of a Vidocq."

Gregory rolled his cigarette thoughtfully, and murmured: "They must make a desperate attempt to steal over in some queer way *now*. It is necessary for them to reopen communication. They must establish a new code of signals, and another cipher, or stop their conspiracy forever. They have plenty of money and use some very smart agents."

"True," rejoined the other as he passed the deal. "My uncle (the ambassador) tells me some of our telegraph corps are members of their order, and are invaluable to their schemes."

"No matter how smart they are," replied Gregory, "the new chief of police is a little smarter. He will ultimately bag them all."

"That is, if they don't assassinate him first," said Alexis, passing over to his victorious comrade a handful of crisp notes (with a muttered curse), luck being heavily against him.

Gregory laughed, as he complacently counted and pocketed the roubles: "The Nihilists will hardly be luckier than you, old fellow! You remember Princess Troubetskoi's pretty salon in Paris?"

Alexis smiled and stroked his blond mustache lovingly, in memory of past conquests.

I wondered if stolen kisses still lingered on the handsome warrior's lips.

"Well," continued the captain, "many a fat package of blue bills of the Banque de France has passed to those jewelled white hands from the 'Haute Direction.' She furnishes transcripts of their perfected plans. I am even told that she has obtained such information as will result very shortly in the capture of—" Here he looked suspiciously at me, lowered his voice, and whispered a few words I could not hear to his companion.

"By Saint Vladimir!" cried Alexis, "the woman the whole force have been trying to capture since the death of our dear old emperor? If they catch her she will be a dainty morsel for the executioner. They say she is lovely as an angel!"

"Ah!" rejoined Captain Gregory, with a longing look upon his Tartar face. "In that case I wouldn't mind being *le maître des épaules* myself." The militaires busied themselves with their preparations, as we were nearing the last frontier town.

"Brutes!" thought I, "I shall soon be rid of your detestable company, with its croaking refrain of intrigue and horror," and turned back to my novel, for I had no personal misgivings on entering Russia.

I was the happy possessor of passports, carefully *viséd, "en règle,"* at the Russian Embassy at Paris. I also carried the warmest credentials to my relative by marriage, Constantine Weletsky, one of the councillors of the czar, once a court page of the late revered empress, now high in favor with the imperial family.

This, with other special letters of introduction, would open to me the "charmed circle" of St. Petersburg; for my daughter had married Weletsky's only brother, Basile, a gallant young officer, who had led a battalion into the Grivitska crater at Plevna, and then had died far away in the Orient, leaving his girl widow with a little fatherless infant.

My daughter had met and been married to this gentleman in Japan.

It was in her interest, and to see her again, I was visiting Russia for the first time.

I had left my wife in Paris. She dreaded the rigors of a semi-arctic winter, and awaited my report ere deciding to visit our child, who had only spent a few weeks with us in America, and then hastened to a new home and strange but kindly relatives on the death of her husband in the Russian service in Asia.

Clanging bells and shrieking whistles announced our arrival at Eydtkuhnen, the frontier of Holy Russia. Here the road changes to a six-foot gauge, so as to prevent any sudden invasion. This forces an inevitable delay in transferring from the standard gauge at the Russian frontier.

Two hours and a half are allotted for the inspection of baggage and passports.

At this town is drawn the line between the domains of his august majesty of Germany, and those of his "loving" (?) imperial brother of Russia. Painted posts in the national colors, double-sided, impress silence, discretion, and political prudence on the passing traveller. This warning is heightened by the presence of armed soldiers pacing on parallel lines a few yards apart. In the differing uniforms of the above-named august personages, fierce warriors glare at each other jealously on their sentry beats, and face about with a catchy snap and wooden jerk suggestive of toy soldiers.

A splendid masonry international station and custom house, with a superb restaurant, on the Russian side of the frontier, greeted my hungry eyes. Madly did I sigh for the last, for lo! hunger was upon me, and mightily did I crave food.

Alas! the line of divided empire was visibly marked by a grillage of hammered iron, which made my passport to "Russia" and "dinner" one and the same.

Guards with sword and revolver belted on stood at the gates, ready to arrest the audacious who might try to run the gauntlet.

A hundred hungry voyagers, we were penned in an ante-room and ordered to prepare our passports and luggage for inspection.

All was grave command and stern discipline, and the necessary delay was so tedious my inner man reminded me forcibly of the neglected "Department of the Interior."

Waiting to cross the gulf which separated me from that blessed repast, I produced my papers and keys while eying the curious throng of travellers. We were all huddled together. Countesses in furs and velvets, pert French maids, substantial-looking burghers, "impossible" dudes, filthy Polish Jews with curls and greasy gabardines, money-changers, peasants, soldiers, and tourists made up a queer human *mélange*.

Haughty officers strode around, ogling the fairest of our lady passengers and ostentatiously clanking their trailing sabres.

Pushed up for official examination, I showed my passport with the American eagle displayed. A bearded colonel, bespecked with crosses and medals, took it. He genially broke out: "Amerikansky— good!"

As he said this I did not regret the five dollars paid at the State Department for the paper. The clerk had inserted upon it the name of my wife, in case she might travel with me, although she also had obtained an individual passport that she retained with her in Paris.

I was pointed toward the baggage inspector and passed. Already several suspected ones had been rejected for irregularity in their documents. They were holding an impromptu indignation meeting. As I folded up my precious "open sesame" to the blessed Russian restaurant, I was happy; my impatient appetite was about to be appeased.

Suddenly I was aware of a sweet and womanly presence by my side.

A rich, pleasantly modulated voice said in choicest English: "I beg your pardon. May I speak to you, sir?"

The lady addressing me was indeed very young and very fair to the eyes of an old campaigner; for, like most old war-horses, I am somewhat susceptible to beauty in women. Dress and belongings bespoke the lady.

As I gazed her manner showed me she was so innocent and inexperienced that her helplessness appealed to a man of the world like myself. Her liquid dark eyes were anxious, her pretty coral lips were trembling nervously; these, with rippling brown hair, ornamented a delicate and lovely, though perhaps proud face, making a rare picture. Her manner was almost childish, but her figure seemed too developed for extreme youth. The swelling outlines of her exquisite form showed to perfection in a dark brown suit, betraying Redfern in its cut and Russia in its sable trimmings.

Pretty hands nestled in a muff, beseeching eyes pleaded under the jaunty little turban, and dainty feet peeped in and out in high Polish boots.

I lifted my hat to the unknown *élégante,* smiling in my exceptional Sunday-school manner, and remarked: "Certainly, madame!"

"A fair countrywoman," thought I, yet the silken "shuba" on her graceful shoulders seemed to have a local luxury in its blue fox lining.

"Give me your arm, pray. We will walk a little

so as not to attract attention," whispered this fair bird of passage, with a light tremor in her voice.

"I hope she will make it short, whatever be the burden of her song," I thought, for I heard the cheerful music of the knife and fork just across the Russian boundary and could see the swallow-tailed waiters flying around; the first "convives" having passed the sentinels at the gates of that epicurean paradise.

"I am an American going to Russia," she began, "to join my husband, who has preceded me. He had one passport for us both; now I unexpectedly find out that I cannot get over the frontier. I don't know what to do!"

As she said this the gentle pressure of her arm thrilled me; her voice had a musical undertone, "like the leafy brook singing away in June."

"I am certainly very sorry," I murmured. "But how can I help you? I know *no* one here. I am only an American traveller, without official position. I am a retired army officer going to meet friends in St. Petersburg."

I brought this remark out with an air of inno-cence. I had passed *"mes beaux jours,"* and knew these little affairs were often very delicate.

"But I noticed you had no lady with you, and as you took your passport from the officer, I saw it read, 'AND WIFE.'"

"Certainly!" said I, perhaps a little impatiently, for the vigorous clatter of the knives and forks showed me that the meal I so ardently coveted was rapidly disappearing across the barrier over in Russia.

Balancing on her pretty toes, she clasped her hands on my arm; looking up, she murmured, with a meaning pressure of my arm: "You will take me over the frontier as *your wife?*"

"Great Heavens!" I exclaimed, "but *my* wife?" For Mrs. Lenox is at times inclined to be jealous. And all the while the hunger fiend gnawed within me like a rat in an empty raisin box.

"I beg you; I beseech you!" she continued, her sweet voice ranging through its wonderful minor chords. "Don't leave me here. I must cross this frontier now. I am already regarded as your wife. Why, they did not even ask me for a passport."

"My wife!" This was a gasp of astonishment from me.

"Certainly; the chief inspector assumed I was your wife. You are my countryman. Take me to Wilna! I will leave you there. My husband is in Wilna and will thank you there." And she clung to me in childish anxiety.

My head was confused, but my nerves were tingling, my heart was beating high at her touch.

Many a time had I stood in before for pretty women in my world wanderings.

A howl from the Muscovite baggage smasher aroused me to action. Our luggage remained alone on the high zinc counter. Nearly all the other passengers had gone away.

The colonel in charge was entering the "salle à manger." He gave a passing Parthian glance of admiration at the beautiful creature on my arm, and murmured: "La belle Américaine."

"You must not leave a countrywoman in such an embarrassing position! Why, they might even arrest me!" This with an innocent little shudder.

I threw my keys to the inspector, gazing at the beautiful pleader at my side in hesitation.

Where was I drifting? I stood dazed while the searcher hastily threw over my Spartan outfit.

The perfumed breeze gently wafted odors of Mocha and good cheer through the guarded gates.

"You'll have to excuse me!" My voice sounded harsh and hollow.

The bearded official cast his eye on the lady's extensive belongings. I must decide instantly!

"For Heaven's sake, don't leave me here helpless," she implored, a look of alarm in her beautiful eyes. As she spoke she quietly handed me her keys. I mechanically dropped them in the open paw of the hungry official.

Then, repenting, I waved my hand in negation.

"You would surely not permit such a contre-temps to stop my journey when the kindness of mere silence will permit it?" she tremblingly whispered, and her wonderful dark eyes plead sadly with me. "Facilis est descensus Averni." I felt, I knew, I was backsliding! I glanced around. If *her* husband and *my* wife would only walk in! No such blessed juncture arrived.

I caught the eye of the "only colonel" fixed, in-quiringly, on my lovely burden. Did he suspect? He must not! I turned savagely to the custom-house man and asked why he didn't get through that baggage quicker.

All this time the great clock was ticking away a ghastly reminder of the passing moments. The in-spector was tumbling over Beauty's treasures in the open trunks.

The riches of her boxes transfixed the official.

I looked with pitiable, inane enjoyment at the assortment of mysterious paraphernalia and woman gear in her luggage. Not being a Worth, a Pingât, or a Jenness-Miller, I can't go into details. I will candidly admit I was proud of the lady's outfit. It was worthy of a duchess in the delicacy of its laces and embroideries, the richness of its silks, satins, and velvets, and elegance of its little slippers, bottines, and entrancing foot-gear.

The very sight of these sent a strange thrill through my susceptible old military heart. I gazed at the lady whose loveliness these garments would adorn. She clung to me, a picture of innocence, beauty, and suspense.

The examination was over; trunks relocked and hurried away to the train. Mechanically I threw a rouble to the searcher, who flew off to his meal like a bird let loose in eastern skies.

The clasp upon my arm grew tighter, and the perfume from her garments floated round me; mechanically I turned my head; her eyes, made more beautiful by anxiety, met mine. Her figure swayed and tottered and leaned against mine. Good heavens! she was about to faint.

To give her courage, I whispered with an insane giggle: "What a lovely trousseau you have!"

We approached the grillage, the fair, graceful, beautiful stranger clinging closely to me, but seeming to gain strength in her step.

Unchallenged we passed the portals and stood together in "HOLY RUSSIA."

## CHAPTER II.

### "WHAT WOULD DICK GAINES SAY TO THIS?"

The door of the grillage closed behind us with a crash, we being the last of the throng of passengers. As this sound came to my ears it seemed to me the little hand upon my arm quivered and grew cold, and the lady beside me started and trembled. Looking hurriedly at her, I saw her beautiful face was deathly pale, but even as I gazed she steadied herself by an effort, a smile played about her lips and eyes, and she whispered: "Keep my keys, please; it will look more connubial." This with a little embarrassed *moue* that set my heart beating.

"Of course we must keep up the comedy, my dear," answered I. But at the familiarity of my address she almost drew away from me, and a big blush chased away the last trace of her pallor. The blush was catching, for the word "dear" set my mind upon my real dear one in Paris.

Anxious to drive such thoughts out of my mind, and hunger giving me the hint, I conducted the fair one on my arm into the restaurant. This was filled with passengers hurriedly disposing of their dinner, as if anxious to get once more *en route.*

There were vacant seats at only one table—the one reserved for the use of the Russian colonel, who was in the act of seating himself.

The head waiter whispered a few words to him, to which he replied with a smile. We were ushered to the private table of this dignitary, who did not seem loth to bask in the beauty of my dazzling companion.

The head steward, silver chain on neck, handed the menu and wine card to madame. She ordered with the easy freedom of a petted wife, and then astounded me again as she lisped: "What would you like—Arthur?" turning a red but piquant face upon her plate and napkin.

How did she know my Christian name? A moment's reflection suggested that perhaps she had seen it on my passport.

Shortly after, the colonel, who was an accomplished master of languages, presented himself to us as Ivan Petroff, and while I attacked the Burgundy, roast pheasant, and other dainties with the vigor the imprisoned demon in my stomach demanded, my protégée chatted gayly with the Russian officer, who explained to us that he was chief of the Wilna frontier division; remarking that he was always happy to see Americans in Russia, for he knew that they would discover with their own eyes that "we Russians are not so bad as we are painted."

This had hardly left his lips when an official stepped up to him and saluted. Then, begging us to excuse him for a moment, our colonel departed.

As he did so I turned to the lady at my side and remarked: "You have called me Arthur. In order to keep up this *petite comédie*, tell me your Christian name, quick, before the Russian returns."

"Certainly," she remarked; "my first name is Hélène."

"And your second?"

"Marie."

"Hélène Marie—beautiful!" I remarked. "And your third?"

"First tell me what is yours," she said. "I read your Christian name upon your passport, but your family name I did not catch."

"Lenox," replied I—"Arthur Bainbridge Lenox."

At this announcement she seemed to start; but a moment after she said with an embarrassed smile: "Then my name must be Lenox. For the present my name must be that of your wife. A false move now would more than embarrass both of us," she went on, earnestly. "False pass——"

She cut the word short suddenly; Petroff was reseating himself beside her.

As he did so he remarked: "I was sorry to desert my dinner, but more sorry to desert you, madame." This was emphasized by a telling glance from his dark Tartar eyes at the newly christened "Hélène Marie Lenox." "But it was a matter of passports that had to be attended to at once," he continued. "We have just, I am happy to say, arrested a *déclassé* who was travelling under forged papers."

"False passport—eh?" remarked my fair companion. "Man or woman?"

"Man," was Petroff's sententious reply.

"Yes; if it had been a woman—a beautiful woman—we should not have had you back with us so soon," cried Hélène, a suspicion of coquetry in her smile.

"The most lovely criminal in Russia would not have kept me an instant longer, madame," returned the gallant colonel, admiration in his eye, flirtation in his manner.

Notwithstanding I was diligently occupied with my knife and fork, I caught this glance, and something of the feeling of a husband coming into me, I turned the conversation by saying carelessly: "I presume this false passport business is an every-day affair in Russia."

"By no means," remarked Petroff; "our penalties for the offence are too severe."

"Ah! imprisonment as well as fine," said I, perhaps a little nervously.

"Yes, imprisonment for *life*—Siberia," whispered the colonel. "Only the most desperate criminals risk the use of false passports."

My knife and fork fell on the plate with a crash.

"Try some of this mayonnaise, Arthur," interposed the putative Mrs. Lenox. "I see you have finished the pheasant, and this is delightful. Colonel Petroff will have some also." And she gave the salad to the Russian officer with such a dressing of smiles and beauty that the admiring Russian, looking only at her, did not notice my loss of nerve-power and appetite together; for these remarks had set my mind moving and stopped my knife and fork.

"False passports—penalties—Siberia—only desperate criminals dare to use them," buzzed in my brain.

A sudden resolution took possession of me. This dazzling woman was making me a Russian criminal by the false use of my passport. The boundary line of Germany was but fifty feet away. I would go across the boundary while there was yet time, and dodge the clutches of the Russian bear.

Excusing myself to the Circe who had lured me into this false position, and who was very innocently but very charmingly chatting to the colonel over the salad, I rose from the table, strode out of the restaurant, and marched for the door of the grillage, now fortunately open.

Germany was within two feet of me. I was passing hastily through, and in another second I would have been away from danger and punishment, when my passage was suddenly barred.

An official voice cried: "Halt! Your passport to leave Russia."

"Of course, I have no passport to leave Russia," I said to him, in my best French. "You saw me enter here from the Berlin train not fifteen minutes ago. I wish to go back to that train. I have forgotten a package. It is very important and I cannot leave it behind me."

"Without a passport it is impossible for you to leave the dominions of the czar," replied the official in firm politeness.

"But I must go. I cannot lose that package."

"Impossible!"

I looked. It *was* impossible! The crossed bayonets of two sentries in front of me told me that.

"However, monsieur's difficulties can be, perhaps, surmounted," remarked the official Cerberus. He whispered a few words to an attendant on the other side of the boundary. The next minute the conductor of the train in which I had travelled from

Berlin stood in front of me on the German side of the frontier.

"If monsieur will give a description of the article, I will find it if possible," said the conductor, politely, "and forward it to St. Petersburg."

There was nothing for me but to continue to lie. I gave the inquisitive guard a description of the imaginary package, also my address, and charged him to be very careful to have it sent after me immediately.

To lull suspicion, I pressed a German thaler into his hand.

"Monsieur can rely upon receiving his package within twenty-four hours after his arrival at English Quai, No. 5, St. Petersburg," returned the German conductor, with grateful eyes at my liberality.

"Many thanks for your official kindness," I said, with a smile on my face and curse in my heart, to the Russian officer who had barred my passage; for I felt myself in the clutches of Russian bureaucracy, and made up my mind to be polite, perhaps even, if necessary, obsequious to its power.

Then I turned slowly toward the restaurant. It was now necessary for me to take my seat at the table alongside of my fellow-criminal and play out the comedy to the sweet or bitter end.

A horrible presentiment at this moment struck me that the end would be bitter, for the first excitement of the adventure being over, conscience rose up and rapped me fearfully.

Here was I—

"With one wife at Natchez under the hill,
Another at home, in Pike."

What would my own dear wife in Paris say if the little adventure I was now engaged in should ever come to her ears? How her honest blue eyes would sparkle and flame with indignation if she saw me permitting another woman to claim her title; another woman taking her place by my side, without contradiction from me—things which my rash step had now made a necessary adjunct to my safety.

Even as I thought this, her farewell words in Paris came back to me.

"You dear old Arthur, remember your susceptible heart. Do not let your military gallantry get you into scrapes. Beware of beguiling females. Remember how you were arrested for smuggling on a transatlantic steamer on our last trip to New York, because you were too gallant to refuse your arm and the protection of your escort across the gang-plank to a pretty French milliner, who gave you a package to carry. Remember what the papers said about your embarrassing position."

Here was I in a much more embarrassing position. In the United States the doom of the smuggler is light. In Russia the doom of the false passport bearer is heavy.

With a muttered curse I returned to my dinner. As I entered the restaurant I noticed Hélène was gazing anxiously at the entrance. Though conversing with the colonel, she was evidently thinking of me, and gave a suppressed sigh of relief as I seated myself beside her. My appetite had disappeared, but anxiety made me thirsty. I put aside the Burgundy and desperately applied myself to cognac.

My putative wife's manner to me was perfection. In matter-of-fact tenderness she inquired: "What horrid railroad difficulty took you from me and your dinner at the same time, dear Arthur?"

To which I muttered: "Luggage and reserve compartment, my own one," assuming in my manner a tenderness I by no means felt; for her persuasive fascinations had put me into a compromising situation both as regards my wife in Paris and the police in Russia.

The gallant official at Hélène's elbow here unbent himself with the courteous versatility marking the high-bred Russian. Hearing my statement, he told me to have no anxiety as to my accommodations on the train; he would have the pleasure of going up the road some distance on an inspection of his district, and he had charged himself with getting the best compartment for my wife and me. A word from him would insure every possible attention.

Then he graciously rallied us on madame's apparent anxiety for me, stating that the moment I left the table, my wife had listened to him only with half an ear, and once or twice, he had noticed, had been on the point of rising to follow me; closing his remarks by a pretty French couplet on love, and laughing: "On your wedding tour, I presume?" as he lifted his glass to the health of madame.

She blushingly smiled at me, and cried, in innocent naïveté, reproachfully to him: "Oh, colonel! We have been married years—and years!"

"I can compliment monsieur," said the Russian. "He has not lost the lover in the husband." Then the tawny Colossus sighed, apparently envying me the possession of the beautiful creature he thought my wife, who, perhaps catching the idea in his mind, appeared so embarrassed that he cried out: "You are joking with me; such blushes are only seen on brides' faces," and continued, to my embarrassment: "You go to St. Petersburg, I presume, for the season. I hope to meet you there this winter."

To this my *protégée* only replied with her eyes, and I groaned inwardly.

Great Scott! suppose the colonel should stay on the train. A cold chill ran through me at the thought. Then I could *not* leave the lady at Wilna.

The first bell rang. Our new-made friend sauntered away on courtesy bent. He was evidently impressed by my wife's social elegance. I had also
tried to live up to my "blue china" in my brief
*entrée* into official Russian society.

Then I turned to her sternly.

"My dear young lady," I whispered, "you are
increasing the difficulty of our position. You have
let this man imagine we are going to St. Petersburg."

"I have not denied it," she replied, with reproachful lips, "because I knew he had seen your ticket
to the capital. How could I tell this colonel, who
thinks me your wife, I was going to leave you at
Wilna? My anxiety while you were away from me
probably makes him consider me still romantically
attached to you."

"Your anxiety," I echoed, "while *I* was away
from *you?*" some extraordinary emotion, half ecstatic
joy, half idiotic sorrow, flying through me; for her
eyes, though sad and reproachful, were beautiful as
a pouting naiad's.

"Yes," she said, interrupting me. "I knew you
were attempting to recross the frontier. I did not
dare to follow after you to plead with you. That
might have aroused the colonel's suspicions; but if
you had succeeded by a miracle in crossing into
Germany, you would have left me in the most em-

barrassing position a lady was ever placed in. I should have been in Russia without a passport; a *"déclassée,"* subject to arrest and confinement by the first policeman that might meet me. You were about to desert me in this foreign land, taking away the passport that is my safety as well as yours. While you were travelling safely toward Berlin I should have been immured in a Russian jail."

Then she said sadly: "Do you think this is the way Dick Gaines would like you to treat his wife?"

"Dick Gaines!" I gasped.

"Yes," she replied, "Dick Gaines, your old chum at West Point in '68. I have heard my husband talk about you by the hour, Arthur Bainbridge Lenox! When you told me your name a few minutes ago, then I remembered all Dick had ever said of you. I should not have informed you who I am until we arrived at Wilna, and I placed Dick's hand in yours; but your nervous anxiety being aroused by the remarks of the Russian colonel on false passports, I feel it my duty to relieve your fears by letting you know that you cannot get into very serious trouble by taking your old West Point chum's wife to him at Wilna."

Relief and comfort came to me with her words— but brought shame to me as well. I had dared to doubt this innocent girl! Dick Gaines was my old military academy chum. Though I had lost sight of him for the last few years, I had heard that he was engaged in some coal-oil investigation at Baku. This made it natural for him to be in Russia.

Perhaps some of my self-reproach got into my eyes, for the lady said, with a riant voice and laughing eye: "What did you think me, an adventuress, a—a Nihilist? Come, confess—what did you imagine Dick Gaines's wife?"

"That is best explained by saying that I think Dick Gaines the happiest of men," cried I, free and confident now.

It would now be easy for me to explain to my wife how I had helped my chum Dick Gaines's wife out of a fix. I looked upon her with pleasant eyes as, passing me a lovely little *porte-monnaie,* she said: "Please buy me a ticket to St. Petersburg."

"You stop at Wilna," stammered I.

"Yes, I stop at Wilna, but the colonel must think that I accompany you to the Russian capital. You remember he imagines I am your wife. I have not dared to take Colonel Petroff into my confidence as regards Dick Gaines," said my quick-witted partner with a roguish smile.

So I stepped out and bought a ticket for my pretty *protégée* with her own money, for the pocket-book she had handed me was full of hundred rouble notes, sending a despatch to Paris also to my wife's bankers. Though I had entire confidence that any explanation with regard to Dick Gaines's wife would be perfectly satisfactory, still I had only dared write my home fairy:

"Eydtkuhnen.  Arrived all right."

Addressed simply, "Lenox, care Drexel, Harjes & Co., Paris."

While doing this the blood burned in my cheeks when I reflected that I dared not even address a letter to my wife till out of the extraordinary complication that had made the Russian police think I had another in the land of the czar.

I also telegraphed the Weletskys in St. Petersburg to prepare them:

"Arrive to-morrow night, seven o'clock."

Then, quite contented in my mind, which I was soothing with a cigar, I strolled into the restaurant, and devotedly carrying a little satchel belonging to my putative spouse, and with her tender clasp upon my arm, I escorted her to the train, where the gallant Russian functionary was standing to see that she was obsequiously welcomed, and shown to the best state-room in the broad, roomy cars.

Here with honeymoon devotion I arranged her wraps about her charming figure, and cried out gayly: "What would Dick Gaines say to this?"

At which she replied with a fit of uncontrollable girlish laughter—which pleased me greatly.  What old campaigner does not like to have his jokes appreciated?

# CHAPTER III.

### MISS VANDERBILT-ASTOR.

ATTRACTED by our laughter, the colonel, after a knock of inquiry on the door of our compartment, entered as the train got under way.

Looking through the window over my companion's pretty shoulder, my first peep of Russia was not inspiring. Out through the Russian half of the border town we whirled, clattering away on that line road traced by the impatient finger of the great autocrat Nicolas. The landscape gradually changed. German thrift gave way to Russian slovenliness. Low rolling hills, gloomy birch forests, lonely lakes, chilly pools, and straggling sedgy marshes made up a dreary picture. Every few minutes we ran by little villages, each a score of squalid log huts, with sad-looking cattle wandering around over the frost-bitten fields. Hulking peasants in dirty sheepskin coats and jack-boots stared after us. Onward we flew; the crows flapped lazily away over the straggling cabbage patches, and a crisp, sharp air penetrated the car. The colonel and Hélène chatted gayly, while I, taking my gaze from the uninspiring picture without, placed it upon the inspiring one within and thought my putative wife prettier than ever.

She had thrown off her shuba, and thus undraped, her figure, though lithe and graceful, seemed to have lost the slight outlines of a girl in the more glorious developments of a woman. Had not the almost childish innocence of her face contradicted it, she might have been over twenty-five. Though talking with animation, she had sunk back on her luxurious seat as if fatigued, perhaps as if relieved from some strain or mental excitement. Noting this, I attributed it to her anxiety to get safely across the frontier, and the worry of discovering herself without a passport under such circumstances.

Meantime the colonel delicately broached the subject of our sojourn in St. Petersburg.

"Americans of your class," he remarked, "always are great favorites on the Neva. You will enjoy our capital, Colonel Lenox, and you, madame, will enjoy it more."

"Indeed," replied Hélène; "and why?"

"Because," answered the colonel, with an affable grin, "we have many gallant young officers in our capital. Balls, parties, sleighrides to the island, with lots of attention from jingling spurs, handsome epaulets, and drooping mustachios, always make a paradise for women. I noticed madame's trunks. She is prepared with the sinews of war. She has not forgotten to bring her ammunition with her in the shape of many dresses from Parisian milliners."

These remarks about luggage set my mind upon a new complication. I remembered the paper tags for ours. They give no separate checks in Russia.

Every trunk of the lady's was billed to St. Petersburg. When I left her with her husband at Wilna, I could see new lies and new prevarications awaited me—lots of them!

The colonel went chatting along. He was inclined to be curious as to our St. Petersburg address, hoping he might have the pleasure of seeing us on his visit a month later to the capital.

As his questions became more pointed, I was surprised at the girlish tact with which my supposed wife parried his curiosity by polite *ennui*. Her struggle with graceful but polite yawns was so unmistakable that our guest, with *"savoir faire,"* observed: "I will go and see if I cannot find a *partie de piquet;* madame needs rest."

As the door closed, turning suddenly to Hélène to tell her of the new complication with regard to the luggage, I got a start. She had suddenly gone to sleep. Beauty sleep, thought I.

Her attitude was a lovely abandon. Her graceful head, supported by a pillow of blue, was slightly thrown backward, permitting a glimpse of her lovely neck, that glistened white as ivory in the sunshine that fell about her through the car window. Her red lips slightly parted allowed her breath to sigh in and out through two rows of pearls. While one little foot peeping from beneath the drapery of her skirt gave piquancy and charm to the alluring picture.

As I gazed, I envied Dick Gaines more than ever.

Such perfect rest must not be disturbed. I saw the poor child needed it after the excitement of the last two hours, and cautiously drawing the curtain of the window partly down, cut off the sunlight from her face, then turned and attempted to take this picture out of my mind by a novel. French, piquant, and spicy as it was, it held me by the slightest thread. From its pages my gaze would go to the sleeping beauty,—this woman whom I was taking to her husband,—my old-time West Point chum's wife. I must think of her loveliness no more. I tried to drive her out of my imagination by not looking at her, by even thinking of my wife far away in Paris; but every now and again my eyes would return to the fair one near me.

After a time, as I gazed, an unconscious move made my charmer's attitude more beautiful than ever. Her rounded arm was lifted unconsciously over her head to support it. The little foot assumed an easier attitude on its cushions and looked

more enticing than ever, for in addition a most alluring ankle in sheeny pearly silken hose was added
to the picture. Her breath seemed to come more
softly between her ruby lips; her beauty was more
dreamy and more captivating. Recollections of
"Flirtation Walk" at old West Point came over me,
and this old campaigner, with the ardor of a first
classman, pressed a light kiss on the fair white
forehead before him, and Beauty awoke with a start.

"A pair of gloves," laughed I, and cried: "What
would Dick Gaines say to this?"

"That you deserved it," she said, echoing my
laugh, "you have taken such good care of his wife.
Why, I feel to you just as if you were—my brother."
Then, catching my eye, she turned away in charming confusion.

Just then there was a noise outside. It was the
cursed Russian colonel knocking at our door.

"You are merry," said he, as he entered, for our
laughter had reached his ears. "Let me join in
your mirth." And he proceeded to devote himself
to Mrs. Gaines with a gallantry that enraged me.

"Here," thought I; "I owe Dick Gaines a duty,"
a spasm of virtuous indignation entering me. "I
must protect Dick Gaines's wife from this Russian
Don Juan's senile adoration!" The contempt of
amorous *young* forty-five for attentive *old* sixty in
such affairs is tremendous.

To head my rival off, I indulged in a tremendous flirtation with Mrs. Gaines, tendering her a thousand and one little attentions of devoted husbandhood with more than a husband's general fervor. I insisted that her pretty feet were cold and wrapped them up in my travelling rug. I refused to believe that she was comfortable, and rearranged her cushions with the devotion of a ten-minute married man; and at each one of these attentions I cried out: "What would Dick Gaines say to this?" in a manner that sent the dear little innocent into fits of laughter, and very much astonished old Petroff; till this gentleman's curiosity overcoming his Russian politeness, he begged to know who this celebrated Dick Gaines was.

At which, being in a laughing mood, I informed him that Dick Gaines was the man who hit "Billy Patterson;" and explained the celebrated American joke so vividly that the Russian colonel was delighted, and every now and then would cry out: "Who hit Bil-lee Pat-ter-son? Dick Gaines, he hit Bil-lee Patterson! What would Dick Gaines say to this? Ah, ha! ho, ho!" and gave out such Tartar chuckles that Hélène and I joined his mirth, and so we were very merry as the lights of Kowno came in sight, and we ran into the railroad station.

The Russian cried: "I must leave you, but we have time for refreshments. You take tea with me.

No refusal, my dear Colonel Lenox. You and madame are my guests this evening."

"Certainly," cried madame. She accepted his arm lightly, while I followed after them, noting that the charming figure of Mrs. Dick Gaines was very much admired. Her beauty had that wonderful charm that draws the eye of the multitude upon it, and as we entered the lighted and crowded dining-room many stared at the passing charms of the lady, and glanced in envy at me, her gallant husband.

In a moment my frontier queen was enthroned at a luxurious table, and after a pleasant supper our host offered the ever-ready Russian compliment, yellow-seal-cliquot, and drinking solemnly to the health of madame, said: "I must not lose you; I can endure *au revoir,* but an *adieu*—that would be too horrible!"

Here was I face to face with a new dilemma. In politeness I could not refuse him my St. Petersburg address. He would visit me at the Russian capital and find me minus the attraction that inspired his call—*i.e.,* my putative wife, the adorable Mrs. Gaines. What explanation could I give him of my bereavement?

The quick innocence of Mrs. Dick saved me. She smiled into Petroff's inquiring face and remarked: "We shall be delighted to see you at the 'Hôtel de l'Europe.' Don't forget the name, Colonel and

Mrs. Arthur Lenox! Put it down in your pocket-book. I—I'm sure you will forget us in a minute!"

The Tartar eyes told her that he would remember.

"Forget you, madame?" said the suave soldier, as he rose. "That is impossible. You do not know the Russian heart."

"Not know the Russian heart!" cried Hélène, with a blaze in her eyes that astonished me. Then, with a quick repression that astonished me more, she lisped in her naïve, childlike voice: "You will teach me the Russian heart, won't you, in St. Petersburg? We can return your hospitality there."

"I shall have the honor of paying my respects to you soon in our great city," said Colonel Petroff, as he tossed his rich cloak over his arm, grasped his sabre, and kissed madame's hand with solemn grace.

At this moment the bells called us to depart. I offered my arm to fascinating Mrs. Dick, and Petroff, with clanking spurs and sabre, escorted us to the train. A hurried farewell, and we were in motion again, the enamoured Russian crying after us: "I shall not forget Hôtel de l'Europe!"

"'Hôtel de l'Europe'—I shall stay with my relative, Constantine Weletsky, English Quai, No. 5, my pretty little prevaricator," laughed I, with a playful squeeze of Hélène's delicate hand. I was so glad we had at last dropped the persevering colonel and were alone.

"You—you are connected with the great family of the Weletskys?" said my companion, contemplatively, apparently not noticing my pressure.

"Certainly; by marriage."

"That will perhaps aid—" said Mrs. Gaines, impulsively; then she suddenly checked herself and cried: "How nice to be rid of that horrid old Russian—you and I." This last in so contented a tone that I blessed the moment we had met, and whispered: "Wasn't it lucky Dick had gone on ahead, and left you without a passport?"

"Hush!" she cried, "the man is coming to light up." Then laid a warning digit upon my lips, and together we sat looking out of the car windows as the guard illuminated our compartment.

We were in rapid motion now, and twinkling lights danced merrily by as we tore past the little villages where Russian poverty gathers the only strength it has—numbers.

A few hours would bring us to Wilna, where Dick Gaines was waiting for us. I looked at my companion; the mellow light of the lamp fell upon her and made her more beautiful than ever. I was almost sorry that Dick was not in St. Petersburg. From the other compartments rose a din and clatter;

the loquacious Muscovite travellers were holding high carnival.

I became gloomy and silent. But Hélène turned to me and said: "Since I have met you I have grown interested in you, my kind cavalier. Tell me all about yourself and your family. I can retail it to Dick; I know it will interest him."

"Pshaw!" returned I, "your history would be more interesting."

"Perhaps," she said with a slight sigh; "but yours first, mine afterward; we've plenty of time. Please." This last with the pout of a petted child conquered me, and I gave her a general summary of my history since I had parted from Dick to go to Egypt almost twenty years before. And she appearing quite interested in my family matters, I explained to her my connection with the Weletskys, and to her earnest questioning surrendered many minute details of my inner life. Perhaps, after all, it was best to be occupied thus, best for my truth to my old-time chum. So the time ran on. "And now, having finished the secret history of the Lenox family," laughed I, "please give me the archives of the 'House of Gaines.'"

To my surprise, she answered that she did not know much about them—"Dick and I have been so long away in Europe," she murmured.

"But Mamie, his sister, you must know about

her," I said; "the one that was such a belle at the Point in '68?"

"Oh, yes, Mamie," she answered; "Mamie has been married for—for ages; she lives in—in Mexico."

"What was her husband's name?" I asked.

"It was Smith—I believe," she said, hurriedly. "Do you know, Dick often used to mention you," she cried, changing the subject. "'Dear old Arthur,' he used to go on, stroking his black mustaches."

"His *black* mustaches!" gasped I. "Why, when he was at the Point, Richard was a blonde."

"Precisely," returned she, giving a little start. Then, continuing rapidly, she whispered: "Dick has been growing gray lately and has taken to dyeing his locks." A moment after she laughed: "Yours look dark enough now. You'll never have to follow poor Dick's example. You have such fine hair," and patted me on the head like a playful child.

Her innocent compliment bewitched me. "What a lucky fellow Dick was to get you!" cried I. "What was your name before you made Gaines think earth was heaven?"

"You mean before I married him, I suppose, by your inflated metaphor?" she laughed.

"Certainly—your maiden name."

"Why, we're at Wilna," she said, for the lights of that town were dancing before us. "Dick 'll be here in a minute."

"Yes, but your maiden name. I should like to think of you as a girl before Dick met you," urged I, in a kind of romantic daze, for we had been sitting beside each other and her conversation had been in whispers, each breath of which had made my heart bound.

"I'll not let you go till you answer," I exclaimed; for the guard had opened the compartment door and announced, "Wilna—two hours."

"Dick 'll see us!" she whispered, for I had got an arm about the fairy waist. "Please—I—I must go to the hotel instantly. He may become frightened. He may go away—I shall not hear—I shall be *lost!*"

"Who'll go away?" I asked, for her tone was frightened and trembling.

"Dick, of course—I must go!"

"Your girlish name?"

"Vanderbilt-Astor," she cried, and sprang from the carriage, while I, astounded at such a peculiar conjunction of American patronimics, gathered up her feminine belongings and followed her from the compartment.

———

## CHAPTER IV.

### BARON FRIEDRICH.

I OVERTOOK her on the platform. She was almost running along, rapidly draping herself in the fur-trimmed shuba. "You seem in a hurry, Mrs. Gaines, *née* Vanderbilt-Astor," laughed I, assisting her tenderly in her toilet.

"Quick! I—I want to find Dick," she muttered.

Surrounded by a number of our fellow-travellers, we moved rapidly toward the porch of the hotel, the Russian air, keen as knife-blades, quickening our motions. Tripping along by my side, Mrs. Gaines's step appeared to grow lighter. As the time for meeting her husband approached, was my sad thought. Curiously enough, this idea seemed to make my spirits and footsteps much more heavy.

The portico of the Hôtel de Wilna was a blaze of light; several richly clad *dvorniks* and porters awaited at its open doors the crowd of first-class passengers on this train, who generally while away their two hours' wait under its hospitable roof; for no one is in a hurry in Russia.

As we neared the entrance Hélène's eyes peered curiously about as if in search of some one.

"Expecting her husband," thought I.

A moment after, a gentleman cloaked and hooded after the manner of the Russian middle classes stepped toward her in the crowd, but, seeing her hand upon my arm, seemed to hesitate, glanced at me suspiciously, and murmured something in Russian, then turned to go. But as he did so I caught a sleight-of-hand movement of his, which pressed a paper into the hand of the lady by my side, which was apparently outstretched to receive it.

"A message from Dick?" murmured I. "You understand Russian?"

"A word or two," she whispered, as she glanced hurriedly at the scrap of paper. The next moment a sudden shiver like that of the ague came upon her, perhaps from the cold night air blowing so lustily about us, perhaps from some inner emotion even more chilly.

"It is bad news!" whispered I.

"Yes, from Dick," she gasped, through chattering teeth. "Take me into the hotel, quick! It is so cold—so freezing out here."

Astonished, I assisted her inside the portals. Here was a large porcelain stove giving out grateful heat. Near this I was about to place her, but the shivering fit left her even before she reached the zone of its warmth. She stepped suddenly from me to the office of the hotel, and gave me a new sensation. In a voice easily audible to the crowd about her, she asked nonchalantly whether any mail had arrived for Mrs. Arthur Lenox, and receiving a verbal negative, immediately said: "Rooms up-stairs and supper for two." Then giving me a smile and lisping, "I presume that will suit you, Arthur," she swept up-stairs, while I hastily followed, to demand an explanation of how Mrs. Dick Gaines expected letters to meet her in Wilna, addressed to my wife.

The attentive *maître d'hôtel* flew past us and threw open the door of a splendid apartment. In Russia Americans are always supposed to be rich, consequently they gave us the best in the house.

"The *Barin's* orders?" he queried, bowing to the ground.

Taking a hint from my companion's suggestion, I directed: "The best supper you can get at once."

He instantly presented the menu and wine card, and, while I selected, Mrs. Richard threw her shuba and turban upon a chair.

A moment after the servitor departed, and turning to my pretty enigma, I said, a trifle sternly: "What made you ask for my wife's mail at this hotel?"

"Did I?" she asked, uncertainly.

"You have forgotten?"

"Perhaps I did," she replied, nervously drawing off her gloves and tossing them upon her wraps. "I was so surprised and shocked at the news that man, an employee of Dick's, brought me, I did not know what I was doing for the moment."

"Bad news from your husband?" said I, with some concern, for twenty years had still left my old chum's memory green in my heart.

"Hush! not so loud! They give *you* that title here," she whispered, warningly. "Come nearer to me." Then she said, suddenly and nervously: "It is awful!—awful!—*awful!*"

"What is awful?" queried I, in a whisper, sitting close to her on the sofa; for tears were coming into the hazel eyes that glistened through them. The shapely bosom was panting wildly under its silken jacket, and hysteria in pretty women always appeals to my military heart.

"He—he has—gone to St. Petersburg!" she gasped. "He left yesterday on business. I am here alone. What shall I do, Arthur; my Heaven! what shall I do?" Then the rivulets of pearls dropped from her eyes.

"Let the experience of a man of the world aid you!" murmured I, an eager enthusiasm in my voice.

With a gasping "God bless you, Arthur!" her panting heart was beating against mine; her perfumed hair was upon my shoulder, and she sobbed.

"Don't! don't!" I whispered, desperately. "What will the waiter think?" For hysterics in women, though charming, embarrass me.

"I—I can't help it," she murmured; "I must—oh, Arthur, you are so good! When you go—I shall have no passport. My baggage checked to St. Petersburg—I shall be questioned—perhaps arrested, and you—you—they may even suspect *you*. You heard what Petroff said about false passports. Into what trouble has my folly got us both! The awful newspapers—Dick will hear!"

Here she had a shiver that was repeated by me; if this got into the newspapers, *my wife* would also hear.

"What—what must I do?" she shuddered.

"Do!" cried I, a sudden inspiration seizing me, "do! Why, go on with me to St. Petersburg—to meet Dick!"

"Of course," she answered. "How foolish of me not to think of that before! I have a ticket. Oh, how unselfishly wise, how nobly thoughtful you are, Arthur!" Then, with a sigh of content like a tired dove, her lovely head fell upon my breast, while in an insane kind of rapture my arm encircled a waist lithe as that of a naiad and enchanting as that of a Venus.

"Cheer up, little woman!" cried I, encouragingly; not that she was so small, but I had got the Spanish

manner of diminutives for beauty from the Carlists
when I served under Don Carlos. "Brace up—don't
sob so! The waiter will bring the tea in a minute."

Thus encouraged, Mrs. Dick revived, noted my
encircling arm, gave me a big blush, started up and
cried quite merrily: "Won't your plan be good fun?
In twenty hours more we'll be in St. Petersburg.
You'll take me to the Hôtel de l'Europe, then hunt
up Dick, tell him our adventure, and what a jolly
explanation we'll have! Oh, you are a genius—a
*good* genius!" And the innocent darling began to
dance about in the greatest joy as the waiter covered
the table with a supper fit for Lucullus, upon which
a moment after she fell with a childish appetite that
gladdened me; for I saw her faith in my knowledge
of the world had made her confident of the result
of this adventure.

But as she laughed, chatted, and ate, I began to
think, and as the embarrassments of my situation
came upon me, I stopped eating, began to drink, and
became glum, moody, and brown-studied.

A moment after, the waiter being gone, she
pouted: "You don't look very much pleased at having me under your charge for a few hours more,"
giving me a petulant glance.

"It is not that, but *afterward*," muttered I.
"Supposing the Weletskys meet me at the station,
with you on my arm; supposing, my Heaven! my

daughter has been telegraphed of my intended arrival, and is at the depot with them. Don't you suppose that she'll know that you are not her mother, though every railroad official will regard you as my wife, billed, tabbed, and passported?"

"Your daughter is in Rjasan?" she asked.

"Certainly."

"And you telegraphed from Eydtkuhnen to-day?"

"Yes."

"Then there is no earthly chance of your daughter's learning this in time to be in St. Petersburg to-morrow."

"You speak positively for one unacquainted with Russia," said I, chewing the end of my cigar.

"I know enough to be positive," she cried impetuously; then, changing her tone, she faltered: "to be positive that you regret befriending me."

"Of course not," I said. But here I gave a gasp, "How about our false passport?"

Then she grew very pale and muttered: "You are going to leave me—here alone—you, Arthur—*you!*" staggered to me and took my hand, and caressed it in a dumb but effective way that made me feel proud as an Indian with a new scalp.

"Never!" I cried. "You foolish child, I only mentioned these difficulties that surround us to show your innocence the pitfalls my experience apprehends —to make you a little careful."

"Careful?" she said, very seriously for her; "don't fear me; I will be discretion." And then, vivacity coming upon her, she cried: "I positively must insist that you drink no more wine this evening. If you do, I'll—I'll get a divorce, you naughty boy." This with a warning upheld marital digit and a pair of laughing eyes that were more intoxicating to me than the champagne I was raising to my lips.

So I threw away care, and we made the end of our midnight meal very merry.

But the ticking of the clock on the mantel told me time was fleeting. I rang for the waiter, discharged the bill, and tossed the obsequious bowing creature a couple of roubles. Noting this, Mrs. Dick silently handed me her purse.

"What's this for?" I asked, surprised.

"For my expenses," she returned quickly. "Mrs. Dick Gaines must pay her own way."

"But Mrs. Arthur Lenox——" suggested I.

"Will pay it also," she whispered. "Don't refuse me. My Heaven, isn't my situation embarrassing enough without making me blush every time I look at your open pocket-book? Take this money. You must, you shall; if not all—part!"

She forced a lot of bills into my hand, then said: "Now I can ask you for breakfast to-morrow with a clear conscience!" A moment after we rose to go.

"You—you don't regret not parting from me at

Wilna?" my *protégée* asked, a smile upon her lips. Then she gave me a mocking warning. "Don't, Arthur! the man is looking. You're too attentive for a genuine husband!" For I was assisting her into her furs with a lingering but ardent solicitude that savored but little of married nonchalance.

A moment after, with her upon my arm, I was coming down the stairs and threading the throng of curious loungers, who gazed open-eyed upon the fair Amerikansky Barina, upon my way out of the hotel.

As I passed the office the clerk beckoned to me. "You will excuse me, Colonel Lenox; would you please register and permit me to look at your passport? A mere matter of form, but police instructions must be obeyed," he said with deference.

Thus requested, there was nothing for me but to write "Arthur Lenox and Wife" upon the hotel book; another awful record in case the true Mrs. Lenox ever by hapless chance gazed upon the page.

At the clerk's voice, Mrs. Dick had given my arm a sudden, startled clutch. Now, as I signed, she looked over my shoulder and exclaimed to the man: "Oh, those passports—those passports! We've shown ours so often, Arthur, it must be nearly worn out by this time!"

Then taking my arm, her touch became clinging, and as we passed out to the darkness of the night on our way to the train, she whispered: "I get so

frightened every time they call for that awful passport. What a dear good man of the world you are,
taking care of a little know-nothing like me."

To this compliment I replied nothing, save by
stroking my mustachios, that are still jetty black—
thanks to an Eastern preparation that I obtained
from Ali Khan, an Alexandria barber, when I was
connected with the Khedive's army—though the man
of the world within me was thinking deeply.

A few moments brought us to the train. We
entered our compartment, and Mrs. Dick sank down
upon its luxurious cushions with a sigh of tired
relief, for the varying emotions of our stay at Wilna
seemed to have been disastrous to her nervous system.

I looked at my watch; we had a quarter of an
hour before leaving.

The cold air was coming in upon her. I closed
the door of our stateroom.

"Thank you," said the lady, listlessly. "I—I am
very tired. Would you mind—hanging my hat up?
Oh! You take *too* much trouble for me." For I
was assisting her with delicate tenderness to remove
her fur-trimmed shuba.

"Can't I do anything more for you?" You look
fatigued," murmured I; as, relieved of her wraps,
she had sunk down upon the cushions again, so
languid and listless that she reminded me of Byron's
alluring Dudú:

> "Soft and languishing and lazy;
> But of a beauty that would drive you crazy."

"My slippers," she murmured. In a moment I had fished from her hand-satchel the two little articles she named, and was gazing in astonishment at their picturesque petiteness, bronzed and embroidered in the finest French taste and art.

Then she gave a sudden and startled "Ouch!" for I had sunk at the adorable feet that were small enough to be contained in such liliputian coverings, and with the deftness of a lady's maid, and with the courtesy of the old *régime* upon which I pride myself, was busy upon the lacings of the Polish boots of my tired charge.

After a second's languishing dissent she let me have my will, and with the grand air of an old-time marquis I stole her little bottines from her and carefully placed upon the delicate feet the slippers that, small as they were, were all too large for the high-instepped morsels they contained.

But, as I did so, two admirable ankles robed in pearly and glistening silk caught my admiring eyes; the blood rushed to my head. With an insane giggle I cried: "What would Dick Gaines say to this?"

When a sudden and cursed knocking upon the door sounded like thunder in my ears and ended a temporary insanity.

As I opened the door Hélène started up with a frightened, wild-deer look. The conductor, gilt-banded cap in hand, stood outside.

"Would monsieur pardon the liberty?" he said.

I bowed in mute acquiescence.

"I regret to inform you I must ask a favor. The train is very crowded."

"Name it," I muttered, the sound of my voice seeming strange.

"Princess Palitzin and her sister-in-law from Warsaw are on the train. Madame has the only large compartment," muttered he with a deprecating bow. "Would madame kindly share it with the ladies, and monsieur coud be made comfortable in another stateroom?"

Rage entered my veins. I was about to cry: "The Princess Palitzin can go to Tophet."

When, with a smile of amiability which charmed the official, Mrs. Dick exclaimed in a relieved and joyous manner: "Most certainly, sir!"

The guard was profuse in thanks.

"I deeply regret to disturb a friend of Colonel Petroff's, but——"

"Never mind," interrupted Hélène, hurriedly, "I am sure you will do the best you can for—my poor banished husband." This last remark with a roguish emphasis.

The man bowed and withdrew.

Something in my face made Hélène laugh.
"You dear, good Arthur," she whispered; "can't you
see this is the luckiest thing that could have happened? As companions of such great ladies as the
Princesses Palitzin, no one will dare to question our
position or passport."

The conductor returned and removed my small
belongings to an adjoining compartment for two, in
which a gentleman was already retiring. For appearance' sake, I left Hélène my French novels and
some other trifles.

The two princesses entered. The guard had
evidently spoken to them of our ready courtesy. They
promptly began to thank Hélène in the language of
their country. To which Mrs. Dick, now grown
bright and vivacious again, smiled and said in
French: "Excuse me, I don't speak Russian."

The great lady immediately used the Gallic
tongue. She then made her gracious acknowledgment also to me. I replied courteously as I could
with great internal dissatisfaction; though I could
see my military bearing and old-time manner impressed both her and her charming companion.
The elder lady was handsome and commanding;
the younger one, apparently about eighteen years
of age, had a very fresh and girlish beauty and that
peculiar graciousness we find so often in Russians of
the highest rank.

"Monsieur is an American?" said the elder.

I bowed.

"And madame also?"

Mrs. Dick smiled and nodded her head.

"I will leave you now," I muttered.

My tone was so sulky, Hélène gave a little laugh, but perhaps repenting of her cruelty, stepped after me, lisping: "Don't be so angry! my dear old Arthur —good night!"

"Good night!" I answered hoarsely. The next instant temptation overcame me. I took advantage of the situation, and pressed a tender but ardent kiss upon two rosy lips that seemed to pant under my mustachios; and then—oh! the blushes on that piquant face.

These grew deeper as the elder princess said something in Russian to her sister-in-law, who answered by a little laugh.

I entered my stateroom. That kiss, still felt upon my lips, had set my brain awhirling. As I sank upon the cushions Satan whispered in my ear: "She is so fair; why not take this joy that is given into your hand?" Honor held me back.

Was it thoughts of two dear "blue eyes" watching for me in Paris, forgotten for the moment in the charms and fascinations of my beautiful charge? No; it was the vision of Dick Gaines in his cadet uniform, that West Point honor for a fellow classman. Oh, we men of the world—we men of the world!

From this meditation I was aroused by a remark in grammatical English, spoken with a peculiar accent, half Russian, half German: "Monsieur is an American, I presume?" And looking across the stateroom saw that it came from my companion for the night, a round-stomached little man with a Teutonic face, small, piercing Tartar eyes, French mustachios, and general barbaricness in the hair department.

He was well but unostentatiously dressed, and looked sixty, though probably not more than forty-five or fifty, as the bluish goggles that covered and concealed his eyes added to his apparent age.

His voice was the most peculiar thing about him, being wonderfully smooth, musical, and insinuating.

I replied politely to his remark, stating with the usual sententiousness and modesty of my country that I was an ex-officer in the American army, and also an ex-officer in the armies of a great many other countries.

"You are a friend of the Princess Palitzin," he said, and then continued, a slight tone of envy in his voice: "Americans have the *entrée* everywhere in Europe."

Rather piqued at his remark, I will put this gentleman in his place, thought I, and rejoined: "I am here on a visit to the Weletskys; my daughter married the younger brother of Constantine, Basile, one of the heros of Plevna, the one who died in Japan."

"Ah! a relative of the Weletskys." His tone showed I had risen in his estimation, as it should, I having mentioned one of the oldest and most aristocratic families in Russia.

"You Americans are a great nation," he continued; and then suddenly asked me so many curious but well-considered questions about my country that we fell into a genial and perhaps intimate conversation over a couple of good cigars; I telling him of one or two army adventures with Indians on the plains, and he astonishing me with a couple of peculiar anecdotes of the inner life of some young New Yorkers who had just visited St. Petersburg, that made me open my eyes in wonder.

A moment after, as I was retiring, he remarked: "I may be compelled to leave the train before you awake; should I be able to be of service to you, please call upon me, Colonel Lenox," and handed me the following:

---

*Baron Friedrich.*

---

## CHAPTER V.

### LA BELLE AMÉRICAINE.

IT was daylight when I awoke. The "moujik" was tapping at the door as a signal for breakfast. I arose to the responsibilities of another day in Russia. While dressing, the conductor came in to take a look at my tickets. , He reiterated the high titles of the Princesses Palitzin. They were the wife and sister of the Governor-General of Poland.

After offering me every attention, he was about to withdraw, when I heard the voice of my companion of the night before. This gentleman had apparently not left the train as he had expected, for he was sitting upon his side of the compartment, and making his toilet arrangements, which were simple, as he had only removed his coat and vest.

"A word with you, sir," he said curtly to the conductor.

"Yes, your worship," answered the man, with respectful bow.

"I don't think you understand exactly who I am," muttered my companion, "or you would not

neglect certain train regulations. A word in your
ear, you beast! you dog! you swine!" And he
seized the autocrat of the train by his ear, drew him
near to him, and whispered half a dozen words.

As he did so the conductor's face grew ashy
pale, his knees became weak, and he grovelled
and fawned and wriggled before my sneering companion.

"Yes—your high excellency—your grand high-
ness—pardon your most humble slave. Pardon."

"No more compliments, but attend to what I
have told you; and, by the bye, you may order my
breakfast for me in the eating-house, and for my
American friend also, who I hope will be my guest,"
he said, with a kindly smile at me, as the conductor cringed and grovelled his way out of our
compartment.

Decidedly impressed with the effect of his communication, I accepted Baron Friedrich's invitation
to breakfast.

Descending into the crisp, electric, snappy air, I
really enjoyed the strangeness of my surroundings.
Mind and nerves were rested after the exciting but
pleasing emotions of the preceding day.

Stepping into the station, I ordered a dainty
repast sent to my wife, and that fascinating lady
forwarded me her thanks and the information that
she would see me very shortly. This message came

by the maid of one of the Palitzin ladies, for these official *grandes dames* were not early birds themselves, and their servant was foraging for them also in the restaurant.

Mrs. Dick being taken care of, Baron Friedrich and I sat down to a repast, over the memories of which, even at this day, I smack my lips.

Every luxury of the season was placed before us. The trout were from Gatschina, the patridges from Finland; the ham was that of the genuine wild boar from Westphalia. We drank Johannisberg of the real imperial stock, and our cigars—even in Cuba I had smoked no better.

Such a meal breeds friendship in man and love in women. Our conversation, which began in the every-day remarks of casual acquaintances, became gradually that of intimates.

We talked with the freedom of old friends, and I was astonished at my companion's deep insight into business, literature, and the affairs of the world. Once I was about to touch upon politics, but he at once stopped me, remarking: "Never comment on government in this country. The more you think of political subjects, the less you'd better say about them."

"But I was going to talk of American politics. What has the high tariff of the United States got to do with the government of the czar?" I protested.

"Perhaps nothing—perhaps something," he rejoined, "but don't whisper about it. Dream of it if you like, but only then if you don't talk in your sleep. Take my advice and remember that we regard a social crime in this country"—here he gave a little grin—"as quite venial compared to a political one."

The authority of his remark rather surprised me; but I was even more astonished at the obsequious grovellings of the landlord of the hotel. He had appeared once or twice during our meal, but as we stepped out to the platform, he bowed and scraped and squirmed after us, and, kissing my companion's hand, begged to know if the meal had suited his high nobility's taste. Could he not put a hamper of provisions upon the train for him; at least a box of cigars and some champagne?

The cigars Baron Friedrich finally deigned to accept, and our host bowed himself away. A moment after my companion turned to me and said: "I had expected to leave you at Dünaburg before you awoke, but some information I received at that place takes me on to the capital. You will excuse me for the present; I have some little matters that require my attention before the train leaves."

Then, with a kindly nod, he left me; while I wondered to myself who the deuce this little half German, fourth Tartar, fourth Frenchman was that

5*

the railroad employees should squirm before him as if he were a god upon earth; finally concluding that he must be the president of the line on a quiet spotting and inspection tour. Some of his glory seemed to have descended upon me, for as I took a look about the station, I was regarded obsequiously by several who had seen us together.

The place was like most Russian stations: restaurant *"à la Française;"* the usual white-walled Greek church, with a huge dome, four little domes perched on the corners; wood huts, framed log-houses, and the crowd of booted, furred, and bonneted villagers and voyagers, with a liberal seasoning of gray-coated, astrakhan-capped sentinels, whose bayonets and gun barrels gave off the rays of the bright autumn sun; business-like looking sabres on diagonal black leather straps completed their outfit. A hardy, strapping, blond-whiskered, blue-eyed set they were.

Pacing the platform, I relished my after-breakfast smoke. Really, in Russia one can obtain the best cigars, the choicest wines—and those of the baron were delicious.

As I smoked I cogitated, and as I cogitated became happy. My comfortable breakfast, united with the bright sunshine and crisp air, braced my spirits. I reflected this affair with the charming Mrs. Dick would not embarrass me. On my arrival in St. Petersburg I would send Hélène to a hotel; then find her husband, tell him of the unfortunate predicament out of which I had helped his charming wife; next relate my story to the American minister or secretary of legation. He would perhaps "hum and haw" a little, and smile perchance peculiarly at Mrs. Dick when he met her in society, or cast a pitying glance at poor Gaines when he came in for his letters; but he would fix up the passport affair with the police. Americans are such peculiar people. They would think I sinned from ignorance or love for the fascinating Mrs. Richard; it would be at best a venial sin in their eyes. As I thought this the day seemed very bright to me.

A moment after, my promenade, which was by the side of the train, was suddenly interrupted.

I heard, "Arthur, thanks for the charming breakfast, and—good morning." Looking up, I saw a little white hand, upon which the jewels sparkled in the sunlight, tapping me on the shoulder. For answer I kissed the hand, and a moment after Hélène's piquant face appeared at the half-open window. "Wait for me," she said; "I must take a little promenade with you this morning."

The next minute my pretty *protégée* was on the platform, more fresh, dainty, and generally irresistible, if possible, than she was the day before.

"You dear, good creature, what a lovely breakfast

you sent me.   No! don't answer me in that way!"
she cried; for I was acting my character of doting
husband again upon her blushing cheek.

A moment after, her hand resting on my arm,
she was keeping step to my military strides.

As we tramped I told her of my plan of action
after our arrival in the capital, and asked her what
hotel she would suggest as her abode.

"Hôtel de l'Europe," she said at once; then
whispered: "But the Weletskys!  They are sure to
hear of this now!"

"Why?" faltered I.  "Why should they know of
this?"

"Because," murmured the lady, "the Princesses
Palitzin are intimates of your Russian relatives."

"They know the Weletskys?"  I shivered.

"Extremely well!  The younger one, the sister,
Dozia, is engaged to Sacha, the nephew of Constantine Weletsky."

"Sacha?  What a curious name!"       ,

"Not at all curious.  It's the diminutive of
Alexander.  How little you know about Russia," she
prattled.

"How much *you* do," answered I.

Upon which she looked confused a moment, and
then poutingly said: "You should be proud of me,
not cross with me.  The Palitzins have fallen in love
with your wife."

"Good Heavens! You have fascinated them as you did me!" gasped I, in such an affrighted tone that Mrs. Dick went into screams of roguish laughter.

"I hardly think our predicament is amusing," I muttered in as savage a voice as I could bring myself to use to the graceful creature clinging to my arm in what I proudly thought was rather a honey-moon manner.

"I—I was not laughing at our predicament but at your naïve confession, my *sabreur*," she answered; then lisped: "So I fascinated you?"

"As you do all others," I answered, and looking around me found my words true.

For her beauty was of that man-catching order that every one turned to gaze at her graceful bearing and brilliant charms. The dull, sodden peasants stared after her, the waiters forgot their errands in looking at her; even the hospitable companion of my stateroom, stepping upon the platform to enter our car, gave her an admiring glance from his small, blue-spectacled eyes, waved his hand, and looked enviously at me.

As he disappeared, Mrs. Dick, in a voice of unconcern, asked who the gentleman was.

"I don't know, certainly, myself," I answered; "but he gave me the best breakfast I have ever eaten in my life, and from the cringing obsequiousness with which he is treated by the railroad people I should imagine he was the president of the line, or at least a principal stockholder."

"Don't you know all railroads belong to the government in Russia, my ignorant son of Mars?" said Mrs. Richard, with a playful sneer. "But the bell has sounded."

"That's so; he can't be a railroad owner," laughed I. I was placing her on the car; the train was about to move; she was standing on the steps, her face turned from me. "However, he's some of the powers that be. He's a baron, anyway—Baron Friedrich," I continued.

At my last word Hélène's foot somehow slipped off the step; she fell back into my arms, always alert for such lovely burdens.

"What't the matter?" whispered I.

"Nothing—I—I am a little dizzy. A slight rush of blood to the head," she muttered.

This was curious, for her face was quite pale. However, I lifted her into the car, and a moment after she whispered, with an attempt of a smile: "I—I presume you and Baron Friedrich became quite intimate over your breakfast?"

"Quite," replied I.

"Ah!" She leaned slightly against the side of the car. "You told him of our little adventure?"

"I never tell stories that embarrass ladies!"

"Thank you," she said, with a little catch in her breath. "I—I am all right now. Leave me alone and I will try and think of some way to arrange the Weletsky matter."

I led her to the door of the Palitzin stateroom. Here she suddenly whispered: "Don't be too cordial with your new friend. I presume his breakfast to you was in the hopes of obtaining an introduction to the Palitzins. Apparently he is of the *bourgeois* class, and would give his head for a chance to kiss the hands of such great ladies. Remember, Arthur, he is not of our rank; treat him accordingly."

With this she slipped through the open door of her compartment, while I proceeded to join Baron Friedrich, who smilingly offered me a superb cigar, the gift of our friend, the *restaurateur* of the station. So the train, with clanging bell and shrieking whistle, dashed on its road once more for the Russian capital.

As the baron was now occupied in looking over a number of apparently official reports or something of that kind, I interested myself as best I could with a book, though my brain would return to the Weletsky complication.

The Palitzins knew the Weletskys. They had seen me with my apparent wife. How could I explain this? I determined, if the worst came, to tell the truth about my adventure with Mrs. Dick to Constantine Weletsky, imagining him to be a sufficient

man of the world to keep from my true wife a revelation that would only do harm and perhaps might
give her pain.

These thoughts were suddenly broken in upon
by my friend, Baron Friedrich, looking up from his
documents, and sharply asking: "Did many pretty
women journey with you from Berlin?"

"None so beautiful as my wife," said I, with
ardor.

"Ah! an enthusiastic husband," he laughed, "a
*rara avis* in our world. Madame's step-daughter
married Basile Weletsky?"

"Madame's *daughter*," said I, correcting him.

"Your wife old enough to be a grandmother?"
he queried, apparently surprised.

"Oh," replied I, nonchalantly, "madame looks
very little older than the day I married her. She
and my daughter are often taken for sisters. You
would think that if you saw them together."

"Ha—ah!" he replied, lightly. "You Americans
are a great race. In you I find a husband of twenty
years still in love with his wife. In madame I behold a woman who is a grandmother, yet looks like
a girl hardly out of boarding-school. In her beauty
and apparent youth I can understand why the husband is still the lover—*always?*"

I laughed off the query in his last word, and
Baron Friedrich returned to his documents.

The conductor shortly after told me that my wife would like to see me. Accepting the invitation, I entered the larger stateroom, where Hélène received me charmingly, and the usual courtesies placed me at ease with the two Russian ladies, who asked many questions as to our American home life. Anxious to put my best foot forward, I took the conversation on myself, and after a few army anecdotes, together with a short description of my adventures in Egypt, Turkey, and Spain, I had succeeded in arousing their curiosity and admiration.

So the day ran on till we reached Pokrov, where the last halt of any consequence is made. Here the elder of the Princesses Palitzin graciously asked us to join them at the table. We accepted, as a matter of course. The telegraph in advance had announced the passing of these exalted ladies, and in great state our party entered the eating-room, every one bowing before us, Baron Friedrich among the rest.

The halt of half an hour gave us too short a time for our social repast. The fair Muscovites were well versed in the latest chat of continental salons, and my putative wife seemed no whit their inferior.

A little later we passed out to the train, and while I conversed with the elder Princess Palitzin, my wife seized upon the younger, and they promenaded, arm in arm, about the platform—a lovely picture that attracted the eyes of all lookers-on, for the young princess was a very pretty girl of a blond type, and made a charming foil to Hélène, whose dark beauty was of a more sprightly order.

"How women seem instinctively to understand such groupings," laughed the wife of the Governor-General of Poland to me, looking on the picture with a slight smile.

Baron Friedrich also appeared to enjoy the spectacle, as his glasses seemed to follow the movements of the two ladies. Curiously, also, it seemed to me that a good deal of Mrs. Dick Gaines's exhibition was for his benefit; when she neared him she seemed more intimate, more confidential with the pretty young Russian princess than at other times.

"By George!" thought I to myself, some pangs perhaps coming into my heart, "she is going to fascinate that old duffer also."

This seemed to be the case, for upon the first opportunity, the Princess Palitzin having stepped into the car, he begged me to give him the honor of an introduction to my wife.

Under the circumstances, I could not well refuse this, and leading him up to her, I said: "My wife, Madame Lenox, I present the Baron Friedrich."

Hélène received him most cordially, and a moment after presented him to the young princess at her side. That aristocratic young lady, however, took little more notice of him than she did of her dog running about her.

A few moments of this snubbing and Baron Friedrich took his leave. Bowing with blinking eyes over my wife's hand, he murmured: "So young to be a grandmamma," and walked away, leaving the young princess laughing at Mrs. Dick's embarrassment, who did not seem over-pleased at the remark.

A few minutes after the train started. As I was passing, Hélène caught me at the door of her stateroom, and whispered: "There is only one way for it. Take me to the hotel, find Dick, and, if necessary, I give you leave to sacrifice me a *little* to your friends, the Weletskys. Sacrifice me just a little to save yourself."

"If this comes to the ears of Dick," I muttered; "he will stand no such nonsense."

"Oh! yes, he will," she laughed. "He is accustomed to it." Then ran into her compartment, leaving me astonished; for Dick Gaines of West Point in 1868 would have stood no such nonsense *once,* let alone many times, with the name of any woman he called wife.

A moment after, Baron Friedrich and I, *tête-à-tête* in my compartment, fell into a general conversation, he once or twice remarking upon the extraordinary youth and beauty of my wife, "for a lady who is, I am told, a grandmother."

And I, inflated by social distinction and the champagne of the dinner-table, and wishing to impress my companion with my connections, told him my wife had been a Miss Vanderbilt-Astor and gave him a little sketch of the New York four hundred.

So the day wore on. The little outlying suburbs of St. Petersburg, garden-decked and splendidly parked, came into view. Our noble friends were preparing for their arrival. Already the great golden dome of St. Isaac's Church was visible. We dashed by the splendid mazes of Peterhof, in whose bosky shades the imperial lover had often wooed the beauties of his great domain, and not—in vain.

Then flashing by Gatschina in its marble grandeur, we rattled by heavy barrack and threatening outwork, and with shrieking whistle and clanging bell the train drew in under an immense vaulted roof.

We were in the city of the czar.

On the long platform groups of waiting friends were on watch for dear ones arriving.

Several porters entered to bear out our small parcels. Directing our trunks to be taken to the Hôtel de l'Europe, I helped the Russian ladies from the car. They were soon surrounded by distinguished-looking friends, all merrily greeting the new-comers.

Then I returned for Hélène, who, as usual, on

making her appearance caught the masculine eye
—instanter.

I was about sneaking off with my beautiful but
embarrassing charge as quietly as possible to the
hotel, when the princess stopped her and politely
insisted on introducing *"La Belle Américaine"* to
her friends.

"You will know them all in a few days; they
are all intimates of the Weletskys," the Russian lady
whispered. "It is but an anticipation." With this
she presented us, and my wife was immediately the
centre of a group, who cordially showered upon her
invitations to their houses, after the characteristic
hospitality of the Slavic race.

Upon this gorgeous scene — for several of the
gentlemen were in uniform—I noticed Baron Friedrich gazing with longing eyes. Potent as he was on
the railroad, court society did not seem to recognize
him.

After a word or two with one of the introduced,
a captain in the cavalry of the guard, I turned to
give some directions to a porter, when a distinguished-
looking gentleman advanced, followed by a chasseur
in gorgeous livery, evidently in search of somebody.

"Ah! Constantine," cried the Princess Palitzin,
as he doffed his hat. "You come to greet your re-
lations?"

"Certainly; I am looking for Colonel Lenox,"

said the gentleman.—It was Weletsky himself come to meet me!

I shuddered at the *contretemps.*

"Behold him," merrily said the princess, pointing to me.

The next moment Constantine Weletsky's embrace welcomed me to St. Petersburg.

I don't know what I said to him; I was confused. In a moment he would meet Hélène! Instant discovery and open scandal were imminent. I tried to telegraph her by signs. She was vivaciously chatting unconcernedly with her new-made friends.

"Please give me your baggage receipt," said Weletsky. "My carriage is ready."

"You forget his most charming baggage," laughed the princess. "I believe she is not checked. His wife, *La Belle Américaine.* Go and kiss her at once!"

"Your wife, Laura, *here?*" cried Weletsky. "Why, you never telegraphed us she was with you!"

"I telegraphed, '*Coming*,' and supposed you knew I never left my wife!" replied I, with a horrible contortion of countenance I meant to be a smile. The gallant Russian hardly caught this last. He stood before my putative spouse.

I tried to introduce them, but the words stuck on my tongue, when, to my joy, the princess saved me from the embarrassment and shame of presenting an impostor as the mother of Marguerite.

"I claim the honor," cried the princess. "Permit me, Madame Lenox: Constantine Weletsky, chamberlain of the emperor, the pet of half the ladies in Russia."

At this the veteran gallant kissed Hélène's hand with old-time grace, saying: "Welcome to Russia. Your daughter is detained by a slight illness at her country estate."

Marguerite was not in St. Petersburg. Thank Heaven! This might give me slight respite.

"Don't be alarmed!" Weletsky added, hastily, for Hélène's face was slightly pale. "Nothing serious; she will join us soon." Then looking upon the beauty of his new-found relative, he cried: "Laura, you are the handsomest and youngest grandmother on earth!" and gave her an impetuous kiss. To which Hélène answered, accepting the name and greetings of my true wife, while I groaned to myself in a fit of unutterable shame.

"*Au revoir,* princess," said he to Madame Palitzin, offering Hélène his arm, and marched out of the station, while I mechanically followed, cursing Mrs. Dick Gaines's attractive charms and her love of admiration that had already made her known to half a dozen of the Weletsky set as my wife.

We reached the carriage; the chasseur had already mounted the box. Here sudden resolution came to me. To permit an impostor to take her place as

my wife under his welcoming roof, and in the bosom
of his family, would be an outrage on hospitality that
at any cost I must prevent.

I laid a detaining hand upon the old courtier's
arm, and said: "You must not think of taking us
to your house. I have no doubt you have very
comfortable quarters *en garçon* arranged for me, but
I could not think of taxing you with the unexpected
arrival of a lady."

"Pshaw! my dear Lenox," answered Constantine,
a little impatiently; "my house can accommodate
half a regiment."

But here seeing something awful in my eye, Mrs.
Dick chimed in: "How kind you are! But we cannot come to your house at present. My trunks have
already been despatched to the Hôtel de l'Europe.
Would you part a lady and her dresses?"

"No," muttered Weletsky. "I am afraid that
might be parting her from her good nature." Then
he continued, evidently disappointed at our not accepting his hospitality: "But you must come to me
to-morrow: I will take no refusal as to that."

"To-morrow," answered I, desperately, anxious
for any respite—anything to postpone the confession
this meeting must soon compel me to make to my
hospitable relative.

"Very well," he replied. "To-morrow! But you

must let me drive you to the hotel; I at least insist on that."

With this he assisted my putative spouse into his handsome equipage, and we rattled away past blocks of enormous houses, arcades, churches, bridges, all sombre-tinted stone. Myriad lights glistened as we dashed down the crowded Nevsky Perspective. And all this ride, to my horror and surprise, Mrs. Dick Gaines, playing the anxious mother, questioned eagerly as to her daughter's health, doings, and occupations. "You don't know how I've missed my sweet girl, Constantine," she lisped. "*You* do not know a mother's heart."

A moment after we were at the hotel.

Here Weletsky made his *adieux,* remarking: "I presume my nephews, Sacha and Boris, will drop in on you this evening; and you, Lenox, if you are not too tired with your journey, can't you come over and see me to-night? To-morrow my wife will call upon you, my charming little Américaine." He gave Hélène another fraternal kiss, then drove away.

We were ushered into the hotel, and found ourselves in a very handsome apartment *en suite,* looking out upon the *Michael Strauss.*

Coming in Weletsky's equipage, and being Americans, gave us unlimited prestige and credit; besides, madame's trunks were in number and size

6 *

impressive to the hotel clerk and wearying to the hotel porter.

These were being arranged in a luxurious bedroom at one side of our parlor; another *chambre à coucher,* opening into the *salon* from the other side, seemed set apart for my baggage.

Looking upon this, Mrs. Gaines remarked, nonchalantly tossing off shuba and furs: "You will excuse me for half an hour, Arthur; my trunks are here. I shall step into the other room and remove some of the railroad dust. You had better do the same in your apartment. Railroad dust does not become you either."

She pointed across to the other room, and giving me a ceremonious bow and little laugh at my appearance, which I will own was somewhat dingy, disappeared to the mysteries of her toilet.

Thinking her advice good, I took it.

Half an hour afterward, in the evening dress of an American gentleman, which I am, happy to say becomes my still erect and martial figure, I reappeared in our gorgeous *salon*, where the attendants were arranging a dinner for two.

"Covers for three!" said I, promptly.

"For *three?*" was echoed from the door of the opposite room, which was just opening. With this, in came Mrs. Gaines, with diamonds sparkling on her white arms and neck and shoulders, that were bare and dazzling, though her evening dress was more that of a girl than a woman, being some white thing that at times clung to her, making her a statue, and at others appeared so light and floating that she seemed a sylph.

"Whom do you expect?" cried she, entering rapidly and coming toward me.

"Dick, of course! I am going to find him."

"Ah!" said the lady, playing with a bracelet on her rounded arm. "Supposing we let Dick wait for an hour or two."

"Perhaps it might be a good idea; Dick has been a naughty boy. Richard should be punished!" laughed I, happy at the idea of a *tête-à-tête* meal with the beauty before me—more happy that she wished it.

Suddenly I got a start. She turned to the waiter and said: "I expect letters to meet me here. Bring any for Mrs. Arthur Lenox!"

The man bowed and went on his errand.

Her continually taking the name of my wife annoyed me.

"You keep up your *rôle* well," remarked I. Then I went on sternly: "*Too* well! You have even taken my Laura's name. You have become known as my wife to my daughter's set in St. Petersburg. This thing must stop, *at once!* I know it will be pretty hard on poor Dick. I presume there'll be some little scandal and talk about you, and a very nasty interview with my daughter, and perhaps my wife, for me; but I am going to hunt up Dick Gaines before the hour is out; tell him how I've helped you out of a scrape on the frontier, and you've got yourself in a worse one here; and perhaps, if the dinner is good enough, he'll forgive us."

Then looking at the luxurious room, the table with its brilliant wax lights, sparkling crystal, and snowy linen, I cried with a mocking laugh: "What would Dick Gaines say to this?"

I paused in astonishment. The servant had brought her a letter—a letter addressed to my wife. This she tore open and glanced at. She turned to me. I saw her face, and the last joke I ever uttered in this world about Dick Gaines died on my lips.

———

## CHAPTER VI.

### MY WEDDING DINNER.

HER face, deathly pale, had warning in it.  She was gliding to the door by which the lackey had passed out.  One quick, searching glance into the hall, and she closed and locked it rapidly but noiselessly.

Then hanging her handkerchief over the key, she swept with sinuous grace to each of the windows, inspected their manifold draperies, drew down the only blind that was up, passed to each sofa and chair and examined; next, lifting the white coverlid of the dining-table, gazed under its handsome oak.

This I watched, amazed and speechless.  The horror of the thing came afterward, as she glided to me and whispered: "I have a few minutes to tell you how to save yourself and me."

"What do you mean?" gasped I.  And as I looked at her, more amazement and more horror came with her movement, for this innocent child, whose dilemma at the frontier I had made easy, and whose road to Wilna and St. Petersburg I had soothed to the best of my masculine ability, was critically examining a tiny but deadly bull-dog revolver. Her eyes had grown bright, keen, resolute, and wary. A peculiar flash was in them—one I had never seen before in woman, but have since learned what it meant. Was she demented?

I was about to break out.

"Quiet!" she said. "Let me speak and save us both, while I have time. I have no husband in St. Petersburg—no husband upon this earth!"

"Great heavens!"

"I had expected to leave you at Wilna, but the message I received there rendered it imperative that I come here, and you kindly offered to take me. This message," she glanced hurriedly over the note in her hand, "tells me that I must use the utmost caution here also. There are spies about us—in this hotel. Please place a cigar between your lips."

Mechanically I obeyed.

"Now I will light it." This she did, using with pretty grace the warning message, and so destroying it. As it became ashes, she continued rapidly: "If I leave you here, we shall both be suspected—both be arrested."

"That will not amount to much. We—we are Americans!"

"You are," she said, "but I am not, though I speak your tongue like a native."

"Then, by Heaven, who are you?" whispered I, getting pale also.

"That I haven't time to tell you. But it is a name they know in this country and fear!"

"My God! you are a———"

"Hush!" She placed her hand on my lips, then went on rapidly: "When I left Paris, I had hoped to leave you here the instant of my arrival."

"When you left Paris you did not know me," I cried, astounded.

"Pardon me, it was necessary for one of us to enter Russia to restore our broken communications and arrange a new cipher," she said, anxiously but coolly. "Do you suppose I would have dared to place myself on the frontier of this accursed land without some plan as to how I would get across its border? Without papers my arrest would have been certain. That you were leaving Paris for St. Petersburg, with a passport for yourself and wife, was known to us. The certainty that your wife would not accompany you was known; also your susceptibility to female loveliness and the softness of your old heart" (was she sneering at me in my agony?) "were equally understood by us. I travelled on the same train with you from Paris to Berlin, and from Berlin to Eydtkuhnen, in the full expectation of being able to cross the frontier and journey on your passport, as your wife, to Wilna—perhaps St. Petersburg."

"My God!"

"Here I had hoped to leave you, but this is impossible.   Hark! I hear a step."

She glided to the door, unlocked it noiselessly, then turning to me, laughed: "Arthur, don't look so glum and so hungry.   Dinner is already here, my impatient husband," as two lackeys bore the same into the apartment.   It was a well-timed remark, for my appearance at that moment, without explanation, would have set a very dull brain to wondering what horror had come upon me.

Then she sat down in airy grace to play out a comedy dinner-scene with me, whose jokes must have been of a deathly nature, like my heart; while one *garçon de service,* with a huge tray, arranged our meal, and the other, a grave-looking man, poured out the "Chambertin" in its wicker basket, and placed a silver pail with the champagne *"de rigueur"* within reach.

The choice wines mocked my parched throat as I poured them down.   I could hear my heart beat in unison with the gurgling fluid, while she sat smiling as one of the panelled Watteau shepherdesses on the walls, whose placid faces mocked my misery.

Mechanically I passed the food into my mouth, and mechanically swallowed it, for my mind was almost a hideous blank, spotted by visions of Dick Gaines—the knout—snowy Siberian wastes—underground quicksilver mines—all done in red and bloody tints.

So this awful meal ran on—soup, *entrées,* roast, salad, a jumble of horror—till my companion said to the servant in attendance: "You need remain no longer. I can pour out the coffee for my husband. I know just how he likes it—two lumps of sugar and one tablespoonful of *kirsch.* Is it not, my love?"

As the lackey withdrew, Hélène passed to the door, and closed it after him. Then returning quickly, she poured out the mocha as she cautiously whispered: "We must remain here together, I still bearing the title of your wife."

"As my wife—continue to deceive my friends, permit you to enter Weletsky's home as the mother of Marguerite? Never!" I gasped.

"You must not, you cannot, *you dare* not refuse me!" she continued, desperately. "Were it known that you gave passport to me to Russia, nothing could save you!"

"You forget the American minister," said I, becoming cooler now.

"Not the influence of a dozen American ministers could keep you from Siberia—or *worse,*" she whispered, growing pale and determined as I hesitated.

"Tell me who you are!" I cried.

"Not yet!" she laughed, a singular smile cross-ing her face. Then she cried: "But you will some day doubtless hear of me."

"Whoever you are, you shall claim the title of my wife no longer!" I replied.

"Pardon me, I have the right to it in Russia," she said, slowly and earnestly, and perhaps sadly, while I stood petrified. "When you transported me across its border on your passport as your wife, from that moment I was known to the Russian law as your wife. The only way of preventing the misery that would come to your true—your first wife from the knowledge of our transactions, is in permitting me to be known as your wife until we can leave Russia. Furthermore, it is the only manner in which you will ever *see your wife again!* For, mark me, were we both arrested to-night, to-morrow morning the world would know you no more. You will have disappeared in Russia. Silence is your one chance."

"Pardon me, there is another," I said, affecting a coolness I did not feel.

"What?"

"I step down to the office of the hotel and sur-render you to the police."

"Ah, how brave you are! To save yourself you would give a woman, who has trusted in your man-hood for her safety, to horrors you do not dream of!" she cried, indignant scorn in her voice and eyes. "You, an American, with your boasted chivalry to women; *you*—" Then, her voice growing winning and persuading, she went on; "I have known you but two days, and I know you well enough to be sure that, with your chivalry and manhood, the course you hint at is impossible."

She laid a confiding hand upon my arm, and all the time her beauty pleaded with me. Then, as I turned my face from her allurements, she continued, a little smile flashing over her mobile features: "Besides, I have made this impossible."

"Impossible?"

"Certainly; you are too much compromised now yourself. You have deliberately brought me across the border under a false passport. You have introduced me to Colonel Petroff, a Russian official, as your wife. You have registered me at the Hôtel de Wilna as your wife. You have permitted the Princess Palitzin to believe me to be your wife. You have let her present me to your host and relative, Constantine Weletsky, as your wife, and you yourself have introduced me as Madame Lenox to the head of the Third Section—*the chief of the secret police!*"

"What—do—you—mean?" This was a sighing gasp, half of unbelief, half of despair, from me.

"I mean Baron Friedrich, the man you thought

was the president of the line, because the railroad officials so cringed to him," she continued, in mocking but convincing tones—"Baron Friedrich, who kissed my hand, and muttered, 'So young to be a grandmamma.'—My Heaven! what did he mean by that? Did he suspect?" she ejaculated, with a sudden quivering of her white lips. Then she went on desperately: "Pshaw! Weletsky's greeting and acknowledgment of relationship, and the Princess Palitzin's kiss put old blinking Friedrich off his guard. What, suspect me, the lady who is even now admitted to the inner court circle of the empire?—Go to Baron Friedrich and tell your Dick Gaines story to him, and see if he will believe you innocent!"

But here, I, who had gazed upon this priestess of despair as if hypnotized, broke in with hideous yellow laugh: "Eternal curses on Dick Gaines!"

"Don't revile old friends," she sneered, in a kind of mocking frenzy that would have been fiendish save that there were tears in her voice. "Forgive poor Dick. I took his name to ease your nervous fears—that would have ruined me at the frontier. Your life was pretty well known to us ere I left Paris, but I only knew your old chum's name; consequently my indefinite reply as to Dick's sister, Mamie, Mrs. Smith, now in Mexico, and my maiden name of Vanderbilt-Astor—Americans are only celebrated for their money; I took those best known in

Europe." Then she paused; her mocking laugh became a sigh, the tears came into her eyes, and this extraordinary being murmured: "Believe me, if you can, that I intended to remain unintroduced to your relatives, to leave you at the station, to come here alone and let you go to the Weletskys; but when I saw those blinking eyes upon me, and heard the soft tones of the autocrat of the secret police murmer, 'So young to be a grandmamma,' I—I dared not leave—the parting of man and wife would have been too suspicious, too peculiar. For my safety— for yours, I thought it best to accept the inevitable. You—you must acknowledge that I helped save you the disgrace of lodging me under your friend's roof as your wife. Now!"—here her mood changed again, her eyes sparkled with all the fervid fire of martyrdom; her tones, though low, were strident—"now I am in your hands. If, after what I have said, you think it safer for *you,* step to the office of this hotel and tell your story, and I—I will only be another— who has suffered death, torture, and shame for her country's cause. If not, in a few minutes they will ask you for your passport and declaration—for you and for me. Make it in the terms of your passport, and I am, in the eyes of Russian law, your official wife." She gave a furious blush, then gasped: "My fate is in your hands—choose!"

Red, burning cheeks and embarrassed manner

gave her new beauty as she stood—the lights flashing on her white arms and gleaming shoulders—with averted head and drooping eyes; one hand covered with jewels that flashed as her fingers played nervously with the forks and spoons upon the table.

As I looked, her helplessness raised all the American within me. I forgot her awful wrong to me. Was I a man that should cast this refined woman in her delicate loveliness to the brutal hands of the vodki-sodden Russian police?

I spoke hoarsely. "Enough! I make the declaration. I announce you as MY OFFICIAL WIFE!"

"Then—then you are not sorry I am not Dick Gaines's spouse?" she asked, in faltering tones, and with a glance full of latent coquetry, which maddened me.

"Thank God! you are no wife to friend of mine," I cried with an emphasis, the *diablerie* of which made her cower from me.

As she did so, a tap at the door, and the secretary of the hotel entered for my passport for transmission to the police.

I MADE THE DECLARATION!

The official left the room, and she, my Circe, stood at the door of her chamber, triumph in her eye.

Then one of her sudden metamorphoses came upon her. This woman of the world's, this political conspirator's manner became childlike. She had been a statue; now she was a sylph, that pouted like a spoiled child, "Now you know I am not Mrs. Dick Gaines, I shall not receive so much attention from you?"

"On the contrary," I cried, "you shall receive *much more!*" As I sprang toward her, Hélène gave a little cry and disappeared. The lock clicked in her door, her laugh came to me from the other side.

What did I care? She could not forever laugh at me. The thousand emotions of the last hour had made me desperate. I could play a man's game anywhere. I would do it now! No doubt a short and merry one—but *vive la bagatelle!*

I tossed off a glass of champagne, and looking at the glass and china and linen of our almost untasted banquet, I muttered hoarsely: "*My official wedding dinner!*" then threw myself into a chair and burst into a laugh that tried to be merry. I—the criminal of a day—the *déclassé*—the fugitive from the Russian secret police—I—the lost—the ruined—the despairing!

# BOOK II.

## A HORRIBLE HONEYMOON.

### CHAPTER VII.

#### OPENING JOYS.

I DON'T know how long I remained in a meditation that was half wild agitation, half comatose despair. Probably a very few minutes. Then a rap at the door started me up. Was it the dreaded Third Section? Had Baron Friedrich suspected us on the train? were his emissaries already upon us? They generally made their arrests at night, I had read in one of Stepniak's books, the horrors of whose pages now came vividly home to me.

A noise came in over the transom.

My Heaven! it was the clinking of handcuffs.

I staggered to the door and opened it.

A waiter stood there with a silver tray and snuffers for the wax candles of our dinner table. To kill time he had been tapping one upon the other, nearly killing me with fear and faint heart.

"Might he remove the dinner service?" the man inquired.

"Certainly!" Here I got back to the table and gulped down another brandy. My drink was broken in upon by another lackey, bearing the cards of Boris Weletsky, a lieutenant in the imperial navy, and Major Alexander Weletsky of the Chevalier Garde.

These gentlemen had called to pay their respects to Colonel and Madame Lenox.

"Show them up!" I ordered. I could hardly refuse to receive the nephews of Constantine; besides, in my present state of mind any company was better than my own.

I stepped to Hélène's door, and in answer to my knock my official bride replied, rather shortly, that she was busy with her trunks.

"To-morrow morning, my dear," she laughed. "See you at breakfast."

"But this evening we have guests, two handsome young officers, Boris and Sacha Weletsky."

"Ah!"

"Yes; that'll fetch you, my sweet love!" I cried savagely.

"It will, my own," she said sweetly.

At this moment the two gentlemen entered— Boris Weletsky in his naval uniform, his brother in the gorgeous trappings of the cavalry of the guard. Boris had a stolid but honest manner about him, large blue eyes that looked you very straight in the face, and a hand whose grasp was from the heart.

7*

His elder brother was as unlike him as his flashy uniform was different from the unpretentious blue of the navy: over six feet in height, with brilliant dark eyes, curly hair, mustache *à la militaire,* and a showy impulsive way that would make him very dangerous to some women.

The usual salutations being interchanged, Boris remarked, apologetically: "I am afraid our visit is ill-timed. You, I can see, my dear colonel, are nervous."

"Good heavens!" thought I, "does my manner betray me so completely?"

"And madame," continued Boris, "is too fatigued to see us. That will be a great disappointment to you, Sacha, as well as to me," said he, turning to his brother with a little laugh.

"And they use the diminutive to you, a giant!" said I, looking at his six feet of athletic sinew and muscle.

"It is the name the ladies best like to call him," remarked Boris.

"Yes," laughed the young guardsman. "My enemies address me as Alexander, and my friends style me Sacha. I trust, colonel, that you will enroll yourself among my intimates and call me Sacha also."

Her door was opening, and Hélène, coming in, caught the last remark.

She gave the handsome mustachioed creature a smile of welcome, and murmured: "And I also."

"That I will, *ma cousine*," cried Sacha, and with the impetuosity of youth and the boldness of a guardsman, he gave "my official wife" a kiss, too cordial to be quite cousinly. This salutation, after the custom of the country, was repeated by Boris, though in a much less ardent manner.

I could see the man-snaring beauty of Mrs. Lenox, *née* Gaines, *née* Vanderbilt-Astor, had already caught the eyes of both, and perhaps the heart of one, of the two gentlemen who stood gazing at her with admiration, as she motioned them to reseat themselves.

"And this is the grandmamma?" laughed Sacha.

"No wonder," cried Boris, with the bluntness of a sailor, "we heard of you, Laura, at the Opera."

"At the Opera? Who spoke of me?" asked Hélène, answering readily, I noted with internal anger, to the name of my true wife in far-away Paris.

"Oh, Palikoff of the Preobrashensky; also Prince Oboresky. They met you at the station with the Palitzins," chimed in the soldier.

"Ah! yes; I had the pleasure of seeing Captain Palikoff and Prince Oboresky, my cousin," lisped Hélène languidly, with perchance a little emphasis on the relationship. "And what did they say of me?" Then she suddenly cried: "No, no! I see you are both going to speak at once. It's a compliment, and I won't take them second-hand!"

"But it is an epigram!" answered Boris. "Old Oboresky will despair if it is not repeated."

"Then, you tell me," laughed Hélène, looking at Sacha.

"He said, 'I have met at the station to-day a woman who, *parbleu!* was beautiful after a two days' railroad journey.'"

"What must she have been when she started!" cried Boris.

"What, indeed?" laughed Hélène, blushing slightly.

"That I came here to see," remarked Sacha, with a profound bow. "And to think," he went on, as if speaking to himself, "if I had not been on duty to-day, I should have been at the railroad station and seen you two hours ago." His dark eyes emphasized this speech wonderfully.

"You would have come to the train to meet me? How delightful!" cried Hélène.

"I hope also to see his affianced, the Princess Dozia Palitzin," remarked Boris.

At which reminder of his plighted troth Sacha gave his brother an awful glance; then his eyes scintillated and flashed with some tenderer passion as they met those of the lady, whose orbs seemed to answer him.

Here I chimed in, not altogether liking these bows and eye glances and cousinly familiarities from the handsome guardsman to my "official wife." The conversation became more general; Sacha giving us the small talk of the court circle, and Boris, sailor-like, expatiating on the beauty and speed of his torpedo despatch boat, the *Vsadnik*.

Then, in spite of me, the party became arranged into two groups, Boris talking to me at one side of the table, and Hélène and Sacha prattling to each other upon a sofa, of which they had taken joint possession.

What their conversation was I cannot exactly tell. A man's mind is not at its best when full of the terrors of a Russian criminal. However, it was of a nature that, beginning frivolously with laughter and jest, soon became confidential, both lady and gentle-man speaking in low tones, which Hélène occasion-ally emphasized by a shrug of her snowy shoulders, and Sacha by glances that I presume he thought killing.

In fact, under my own indignant eyes, it seemed to me that, for a new-made official bride, the lady was indulging in a very rapid flirtation.

During this, as well as my feelings would permit me to comprehend, Boris told me several interesting items of my daughter's life in Russia; also some anecdotes of Constantine Weletsky, whom he called "the noblest old Russian left from the reign of Alexander Second," and said: "You'll love him as well as we do when you know him as well."

Then this young gentleman arose to go, probably noticing my preoccupation, which he attributed presumably to Sacha's behavior with my wife, as he gave that gentleman a reproving glance; also possibly not finding my conversation as interesting as his brother did that of the lady seated beside him on the sofa. As Boris arose, however, he gave me some information that startled me.

"Perhaps you have not heard," he remarked, "that Marguerite leaves her estates in Rjasan the day after to-morrow?"

"My daughter leaving the day after to-morrow?" I ejaculated, starting up, with an agitation that he mistook for joy.

"Yes; she'll be here in three days. I thought it would make you happy. You have not seen her for nearly two years," he said, preparing to resume his hat and cloak.

His hint for departure was taken rather sulkily by Sacha, who arose reluctantly, saying: "To-morrow I shall call again, *ma cousine,* and hope to show you the delights of St. Petersburg. I shall come alone: no brother shall be with me, impatient for the joys

of the baccarat tables at the Yacht Club; consequently I hope to remain longer."

"Baccarat tables at the Yacht Club—that is *your*
passion, Sacha," rejoined Boris. Then turning to me,
he remarked: "Constantine has placed your name
up at that institution. We may expect to have many
pleasant times together, colonel." With this he gave
me a grip of the hand, and madame a cordial bow.
The grip of the hand was repeated by Sacha to me,
but to madame he gave another cousinly kiss, for
which I cursed him under my breath, though too
much agitated at the certain discovery my daughter's
visit to St. Petersburg would bring to me and the
woman standing beside me to devote much time
to discussing this new phase in my official honey-
moon.

The young men's parting steps died away. I
turned savagely upon Hélène, and whispered: "You
have again dared to answer to Laura, the name of
my wife."

"Pardon me," she said. "It is necessary to our
safety that I should answer to her name; but if you
are going to get angry, Arthur, please close the door.
You might raise your voice, and our discussion bring
ruin to us both."

I gave the door a bang, and said, sarcastically:
"I presume you would like me to call you Laura
also?"

"It would be safer," she said; "*much!* But perhaps you may compromise with your conscience by styling me madame, or, if you call me Hélène, telling your relatives that it is your pet name for your wife."

"Conscience!" cried I. "What has conscience to do with the matter?"

She grew confused at this, and muttered: "I hope it has in—in your case."

"It has," I said, scornfully, "with regard to others. To-morrow, the wife of Constantine Weletsky will come to visit you. To-morrow we shall be entertained under his roof. There you will be honored as my wife—as the mother of my child. That shall never be, until I have explained the whole matter to Constantine Weletsky himself."

"That will be your ruin or his," answered Hélène suddenly. "He would be compelled, as an officer of the government, as a subject of the czar, to reveal everything to the police authorities on the instant. Failing to do this, he would become criminal with us. Discovered, his name would be crossed from the list of the nobility, his estates confiscated. Tell him our story—there are but two courses before him. One is to inform the police and destroy you, his relative and guest; the other is, for your sake, to prevent your punishment, to withhold it. If he does the first, we are both lost. If he chooses the second, discovery means ruin to him also."

The truth and logic of her remarks were palpable. Under these circumstances, for Weletsky's own sake and safety my lips must be closed to him.

"So you are not going to inform upon us just yet!" she said, in a mocking tone. "I am still to be your official wife for a day or so."

"No!" I cried; "not for half an hour more. My honor will not permit this deception to continue."

I was getting nearer to the door. I took my hat in my hand. I was putting on my overcoat.

She had grown very pale.

"Where are you going?" she gasped.

"To our friend, our mutual friend, Baron Friedrich," I jeered, gaining the door of the apartment.

As I did so, her voice, that had been excited, became soft and sad—and came faintly to me.

She said: "Then, before you go—please bid me good-by and forgive me, for this is the last you will ever see of me——"

"The last——"

"Certainly! *You* will not be permitted to leave the police-station. *I*—I shall be in the underground cells across the river. Forgive me—I—I forgive you. I am the last woman you will ever speak to upon earth; you are the last man whose hand I shall ever clasp in this world—the hand that sentences me."

She had my hand in hers now; for I had left the door at her words, which were not of a nature to increase my desire to see Baron Friedrich.

"And you," she went on, "whatever they do to you—no matter the torture, the despair—you—you will forgive me who brought you to the shambles, the gallows!"

"Yes," I sighed, and sank down upon the sofa.

"You—you were jealous of me. I was not distant enough to the major of the Garde. Pough!" she whispered. "Do you suppose I care for him or any other Russian—save for his ruin and despair—I whose mother was——"

She checked herself suddenly and went on haughtily: "My family affairs would not interest you; my political ones—your peculiar relation to me gives you a right to know; in fact, are vital to your safety, in case you do not finish the affair by a visit to Baron Friedrich to-night. The communication between the circles of our order in Russia and our organizations in the outside world have been cut off by the secret police, who have discovered our cipher and means of carrying despatches across the border. If we cannot act together our cause is at an end. To arrange a new cipher and other means of communication, I have taken my life in my hand and reached St. Petersburg by assuming a relationship to you of which you apparently would take advantage."

"You have my life—am I to have nothing in return?" I whispered, hoarsely; for in all this interview we spoke under our breaths, fearing the very walls as spies.

"And for it you would take my honor!" she answered, growing noble and commanding, but oh, so beautiful! "My life is my country's; so is my honor if need be. I am defenceless against you, because I have not yet fulfilled my mission. If you betray me to the police to-night, I shall be unable to deliver the new cipher and new instructions to our order here; our cause is postponed, perhaps lost. Therefore, I am in your hands—helpless—defenceless. If you are a man, be merciful. If you are a coward, *take what the gods have given you!*"

She looked me straight in the eyes, then swept into her room with the face of a Boadicea going to endure the Roman rods, leaving the portals wide open.

I arose, the good and evil fighting within me. Then I staggered to the door leading to the hallway.

I had got it half open, when she was at my side whispering: "You go to Baron Friedrich's?"

"No; to the Yacht Club!" I gasped.

"God bless you!" she cried. "I knew I could trust an American gentleman."

Then somehow I got away, and reached the offices of the hotel, at this late hour in the evening

partially deserted by loungers and attendants. I
had passed through it but three hours before, on
my way from the station, excited, worried perhaps,
but not as I was now.

Everything seemed changed to me. The haunting terrors of suspicion, the miserable anxieties of
a fugitive from justice—Russian justice—were upon
me; the terrors of its awful punishments had become known to me by fearful Nihilist novels and
the daily dished up newspaper sensations of the outside world for the last two generations in regard to
Muscovite barbarity.

The clerk at the office smilingly asked me if I
had lost any luggage.

He had noted my nervous manner. Was this
question one to draw me out? Was this polite
creature one of the agents of the Third Section?

"No-o!" I stammered; then, recovering myself, I
asked to be directed to the Yacht Club.

Impressed by the mention of this most exclusive
establishment, he placed me in charge of a *valet de
place.*

We descended the stairs; two hall porters bowed
to me and said a few words to each other in Russian,
then looked after my retreating form. Could they
be spies also? Everything was now suspicion and
terror.

In the courtyard my attendant soon found me a

carriage. As he extended his hand for his tip he bowed to the ground before me. I thought there was suspicion in his look. The very yell of the driver of the vehicle made me start.

A few minutes' rattling between the granite buildings of the Nevsky gave me time to compose myself. I soon found myself on the Grand Morskaja, and at the doors of the most fashionable club in St. Petersburg—as well as the most hospitable to those permitted to enter its doors.

My card of admission was waiting for me, thanks to the forethought of Constantine Weletsky. In a few minutes I was in that luxurious apartment devoted to the highest play and the most reckless gambling in Europe—probably in the world; for the American Indian will only stake his horse and blankets and gun, his wife and his whole family, but the Tartar will peril his very soul as well upon the roll of a die or the turn of a card.

The room was dotted over with gorgeous uniforms, some of which glittered with orders gained in two, perchance three, wars; this dazzling effect being toned down by a few unpretentious diplomatic costumes, a sprinkling of ordinary evening dress suits, and one or two uniforms of navy blue.

Among these I easily caught sight of Boris, who, coming up to me with ready and cordial hospitality, cried out in sailor voice: "Madame was fatigued, eh?

So you have come down to make a night of it with us? Sacha is already engaged"—he glanced at the baccarat table where his brother was playing in reckless, excitable Slavic manner—"so I shall present you to our friends. You are already known by reputation; your wife has made you famous."

With this he introduced me to a crowd of the celebrities and fashionables of St. Petersburg, who were very cordial and hospitable to the American colonel who had brought the coming belle of the winter season—so they said in their barbaric, complimentary way—"to make Paris desolate and St. Petersburg happy."

With these gentlemen, cigars *ad libitum,* and iced champagne—the favorite drink of the Northern capital—*ad nauseam,* I contrived to make a wild and desperate night of it. I drowned anxiety in dissipation and quieted my nerves by nicotine. Then I risked a few roubles at the table and won, and soon, with that peculiar luck that comes to men in certain desperate stages of their careers, had heaped enough *billets de banque* in front of me to permit me a very extravagant life for the next few days.

"My dear colonel, come and bring me American luck; the Russian article has deserted me this evening," cried Sacha from his end of the table, where fortune had been dealing unkindly with him.

A moment after he sneered: "Lucky at cards, unlucky at love."

"Then, Sacha," cried a young man sitting beside him, "you should never dare the baccarat table after the ballerina deserted a grand duke at your nod."

"No more I will!" he cried, and with a muttered curse threw down the cards.

A few minutes after, I left the table, where the conversation, now his back was turned, indicated to me that Major Sacha Weletsky had the reputation, even in this licentious capital, of being about the most confirmed as well as the most successful rake that had ever rode in the Chevalier Garde past the czar, and that is saying a great deal for a young man not over twenty-eight.

"You should give up the fickle goddess," remarked Boris to his reprobate brother. "If you play so recklessly it may come to the ears of the czar, who does not like his officers to become too notorious at the card table."

"Pish!" cried Sacha. "No gentleman here would report me, and as for the servants——"

"Half of them are spies," interrupted Boris. "So be careful."

At the word "spies" my anxieties and terrors came upon me again. I attempted a laugh, and remarked: "I suppose Baron Friedrich himself sometimes drops in on you here?"

"What! that *canaille?*" cried Alexander, wine having apparently made him thoughtless. "He could no more enter here than he could the gates of heaven—save on official business, and by order of the czar. The Imperial Yacht Club does not admit German *parvenus* within its doors, even if they are expert policemen. Ah! Platoff has taken the blank. I always win from that Cossack." And Sacha returned to baccarat again, Boris remarking he would walk as far as the hotel with me.

As we passed out of the club, the dusk of morning fell upon our steps.

The sailor-lieutenant accompanied me to the door of the De l'Europe, chatting with the freedom of a relative, chiefly of his brother.

"He is very wild," he said. "We all hope his marriage will quiet him. You saw his *fiancée* on the train, I believe, the Princess Dozia Palitzin—a lovely girl, very young and a great heiress. But Sacha neglects even her, running after every new and beautiful face; sometimes, I am sorry to say, with too much success."

Was this intended to warn me to guard my official wife from this military Lothario? Apparently not, as the sailor immediately turned to society topics; telling me of the great ball that the Countess Ignatief was about to give, for which he should exert himself to obtain for us cards. "That will be comparatively easy," he said. "The countess makes a point of having all great beauties at her *fêtes.*"

Here he was suddenly interrupted; a half-dozen men, un-uniformed, crossed the street rapidly in front of us and passed down a smaller one running at right angles out of it.

We reached the corner and I looked after them. They were before the door of a house, that opened to them in a moment. As they entered, the noise of distant struggle, mingled with a woman's cries, came to me.

"A fire!" I exclaimed, and was about to run to it, *à l'Américaine,* when Boris's clutch was on my arm.

"We're not wanted there," he said, significantly; "it is a police affair."

"A-ah, some crime—murder, perhaps!" answered I, for a closed van was drawing up in front of the house, and into it two men and a woman, all bound and silent now, were being thrown.

"Come away," said Boris, hastily, and we moved on. "If it is a murder, you'll read the official report of it to-morrow; if it is what I imagine——"

"I'll read?"

"Nothing!"

"Why, in America there would be twenty reporters on the spot by this time, and big head-lines in to-morrow's papers."

8*

"American journals wouldn't last long in this country—nor American reporters either," said the lieutenant in a very signifiant tone, one that set me to thinking and my nerves to quivering.

Noting my preoccupied manner, my companion said but little. We were soon at the hotel, and, with a cordial grasp of the hand, this honest young Muscovite sailor left me.

I went upstairs, and, entering my apartments with a pass key, found the *salon* as I had left it. The lights were turned down; Hélène's door was open wide. Should I take a peep at sleeping beauty? Curiosity overcame resolution; I looked in.

Great heavens! the bed had not been used, the room was empty. With a gasp of dismay, I sank into a chair. What had happened?

Recovering from the shock, my mind began to act. I made a hasty search; her boxes, trunks, and band-boxes were there, even her jewels, but no Hélène.

Where had she gone, what had happened to her? Had she attempted to communicate with her order —had she been arrested? My heavens! was she the silent woman I had seen thrown like a trussed-up lamb into the police-van?

I shuddered at this, not for my own fate, but for hers; for in all this affair one astonishing part of it was that I never grew angry at her for the risk she had placed upon me, though often ready to destroy her for her coquetries, that drove me mad with impotent jealousy.

A few seconds' thought convinced me my only course was inaction; to announce her absence to the office of the hotel would be more than dangerous.

It would appear more innocent in me, in case of trouble, to know nothing of Hélène's being out. I slipped into my own room, hastily threw off my clothes, and, creeping into bed, waited with anxious ears for Hélène's coming steps.

But after a little the generous draughts of Yacht Club Cliquot began to affect me; I grew drowsy, and fell into a sleep, to dream of horrors I shall remember while life lasts. Great Scott, what an official honeymoon!

## CHAPTER VIII.

### I LUNCH WITH BARON FRIEDRICH.

A TAPPING on my door awoke me; a fresh voice was crying: "Arthur, what are you dreaming about? Your groans will arouse the hotel!"

I arose with a start. What was the matter with me? The sun was shining brightly in my window. What ghastly thing was hanging over me that made my waking from that awful dream only a respite?

"Arthur!"

*Her* voice—I knew! I sprang from the bed as if it had been electrized, for I remembered.

"Arthur, my dear!"

"What is it!" I called.

"Breakfast, my love. You're awfully late—the trout are growing cold," cried my spouse *pro tem.*

A hasty toilet, and I stepped out to meet the embarrassments, perplexities, and dangers of the day, that stood awaiting me embodied in the graceful form of "my official wife," who sat, a tantalizing but domestic picture, pouring out tea at the foot of a table covered with an appetizing breakfast.

She was in a piquant, coquettish morning wrapper, or tea-gown, or demi-toilet, or whatever women call those extraordinary yet fascinating gowns that make them more graceful, more insinuating, more torturing to the man they hold at a distance than all the glory of full-dress regalia. I seated myself at the table, and found in front of me my ticket *de séjour*, permitting a three weeks' stay in the capital.

"You never kept me waiting so long before, dear Arthur," she said, sweetly. "I have so much to do; so much depends—o-oh!"

I had played my part of doting husband for the benefit of the servant and sealed her lips, she not being able to expostulate violently without ruin to teacups and saucers.

For a moment she looked haughty, then blushingly turned to the waiter and said: "We have everything that is required."

The man withdrew grinning. He thought she wished another salute.

She cried: "Arthur, see that the door is shut! Ough! the draughts."

This I did, taking a surreptitious squint to be sure that our waiter was not at the key-hole.

As I returned to the table, she whispered: "What was the meaning of those awful outcries in your sleep? You would have had every one in the hotel here had I not awakened you."

"Madame," I said, savagely, "I was dreaming we were arrested and I was suffering the punishment of the knout—for *your* sake!" I put such an insinuating pathos in the last phrase that she went into hysterical laughter and made me more angry with her than ever.

Recovering from this, she whispered: "Dreams go by contraries." Then, becoming very serious, she said: "We must consult together how to avoid such an awful catastrophe. Sit down near me; while we breakfast we can discuss the matter."

As I did so I remarked to her, under my breath: "You were out last night—where?"

"That," she replied, "for your own sake, I will not tell you. To know the details of this business upon which I am engaged would only add to your embarrassment were I discovered—only increase your punishment were we arrested. It is sufficient that I have advanced my business very much, and no suspicion rests upon me in the office of the hotel, where they suppose I have been on a visit to the Weletskys. Won't you have some trout? They are very delicious."

"No, thank you," replied I, sulkily.

Then she went on between bites, trouble apparently rather sharpening her appetite: "A thousand embarrassments are upon us. — Some coffee, darling?"

"No," I said, glumly, to the last, then queried to the first: "New ones?"

"Yes, these." She held up a number of letters. "We must make up our minds exactly how to act; then, having taken our line, stick to it. Am I to enter Russian society or not?" She tossed half a dozen invitations, cards, etc., in front of me, most of them bearing distinguished names. Among them was an invitation to the Ignatief ball, which was enclosed with a card of the Princess Palitzin. Apparently to her good offices we owed the compliment.

"If I refuse these and do not go out in the world it may be thought, not unnaturally, suspicious. If I accept them, we bring upon us all the dangers of great publicity. Which do you advise?"

"How long do you remain here?" asked I.

"Until I have finished my work."

"Which means?"

"At the most, three days, though I have advanced so much that it may be ended this afternoon."

"And at the end of that time you will be ready to leave Russia—you will leave Russia as soon as I find a way to get out of it?" said I, impressively.

"Yes; but can you do this? The way into the rat-trap is easy—but to get *out!*" She shrugged her shoulders.

"To do this there must be no suspicion on us," I said, seriously.

"I must write to my wife in Paris, otherwise perplexing telegrams may come."

She replied: "You must do that, at once."

"Under cover to my bankers in Paris by means of the American Embassy," I answered, then suddenly cried:

"But my daughter? She will be here in three days."

"She must not be here in three days."

"How can I prevent it?"

"Telegraph her. You can safely telegraph Marguerite; you have no official daughter with you in St. Petersburg," she said, playfully. "Now, as to society. It will be impossible for me to refuse to receive Madame Constantine Weletsky; equally impossible for me to neglect to visit her. If I accept her invitations, I must accept those of others. A perfect freedom and ease of movement will be our best protection from suspicion."

"Do as you please," growled I; "I am in the rat-trap." Then I gave her all the information possible about my daughter Marguerite; the very delicate matters of the division of the estate that had brought me as her envoy to St. Petersburg, and other little points that would aid my co-conspirator in playing the *rôle* of Mrs. Lenox; charging her to beware of questions about America, to parry rather than answer them, and not to talk too much about her ancestors, the Vanderbilt-Astors, nor anything she didn't know all about. "You women always ruin yourselves by too much *finesse,*" I said, oracularly.

At which my pupil gave me a sly smile and murmured: "Thank you, dear Arthur, for teaching me to be as wise as you. Now, another point. Will it not be curious if you leave St. Petersburg so suddenly—without seeing your daughter, without settling her affairs?"

"I shall see my lawyer to-day, get Marguerite's legal matters in hand, and finish them as soon as possible," answered I, and rose to go on my errands.

In a few minutes official Mrs. Lenox tripped down-stairs with me, and we were on the "Nevsky." At the nearest principal square Hélène selected one of several closed carriages, conversing a few moments in Russian with the driver.

"Let me order all. I will explain as we go along. I know the city. We have a trusty man now!" Calmly directing the driver to the American Legation, my fair guardian seated herself on the cushions. At the legation I sent in my card, and was ushered into the office of the acting "Chargé d'Affaires." The minister was absent, as usual. Leaving cards for that dignitary, I received a letter from Paris that gave me an awful pang, though I thrust it into my pocket unopened. I informed the

Secretary of Legation of my status, and showed my credentials.

"In what can I serve you, colonel?" was his polite remark.

I spoke of my desire to send letters under cover out of Russia in the legation bags.

"I regret you have asked the one thing I cannot do for you," said the secretary. "Some of the smaller legations have been suspected of yielding to high bribes to convey Nihilist correspondence. The 'doyen' of the diplomatic corps, on our joint pledge, assured Monsieur de Giers that no private letters should be sent in any of our despatch bags. On that express agreement, we saved our legation privilege of using our sealed bags. I can receive and keep for you all your incoming letters. That is not our responsibility."

He offered every other civility, giving me a letter to a lawyer of standing, which I requested. I thanked him and withdrew.

"What has happened?" asked my companion, looking at my face as I rejoined her in the carriage.

I told Hélène of my trouble about the letters.

"Leave the letters to me," she said, cheerfully; then cried to our driver: "To the telegraph office! Quick!"

From there I wired to my daughter, announcing my arrival. I gave my address as "U. S. Legation," adding: "Write only to me here. Wait where you are. I will come and visit you myself. Letters explain."

I felt that I had closed one avenue of danger. I knew the Weletskys would delicately leave all writing to me, as my daughter's business interests were in my hands.

"Now, madame," said I, "I wish to read my— my letter from Paris," this with a gulp, "and answer it, if I can safely. I will also write to my daughter."

"You shall, with security," said Hélène, confidently.

She gave an address to the coachman; he started, and nodded significantly. Through the picturesque streets, crowded with every costume of Europe and Asia, we whirled. Gentlemen in English Piccadilly "form," ladies *"en Parisienne,"* dandy Guardsmen, wild Circassians, silver inlaid cimeters at their belts; Persians, peasants, Jews, Poles, servants, and soldiers, Cossacks pricking about on their hardy ponies, and other strange figures made up a queer *mélange*. It is only seen elsewhere in the world at the bridge at Constantinople, or in the old "Mouski" at Cairo.

I noticed our driver took very circuitous routes, driving now fast, now slow. We passed the great Kazan church, the stupendous golden-domed "St. Isaacs;" many palaces, squares, barracks, granite-balustraded canals, monuments, and temples. From time to time our Jehu looked around, as if choosing a way. Finally we rolled swiftly into a side street, certainly two miles from the telegraph office. We stopped then before a small shop, with a couple of show-windows. It bore the unpretentious sign:

> *"Le Brun.    Modes de Paris."*

"Return in two hours," said my directress to the driver, adding a few directions. "Follow me," whispered my lovely guide. She covered her face with a heavy veil, gliding up the steps swiftly. I descended. A glance assured me no one was in the street, near enough to see. My driver whipped up and disappeared around a corner. I entered the store.

My wife was saying to a neat-looking French-woman: "I require a robe for the Comtesse Ignatief's ball; it must be ready in three days; can you do it?"

"Before that, if madame chooses," answered the woman, respectfully. Then Hélène whispered something I could not catch; the milliner pointed to a side door. Hélène took me into a small room, comfortably furnished. I was a little puzzled.

"Here," said my official wife, "are your writing

materials. Now, get your letters ready at once, while I select my robe."

"But you've got lots in your trunks," suggested I.

"But require another—a woman's caprice. Don't ask questions, and don't go to the door," cried my enigma, and left me with a horrible suspicion in my mind. I was in a Nihilist haunt.

I wrote to my wife—my dear wife in Paris—in answer to her kind note received at the legation. I —I believe I cried over it. I know my answer was misspelled, ungrammatical, but to the point.

I directed my absent loved one to write to no one but me on the impending business, and to cover all her letters to the legation. I forbade her to telegraph, as all messages were at the mercy of the government. I asked her to send her letters for her daughter to me personally, so I could follow the business of the estate. I described my kindly reception by the Weletskys, but said I would make a full preliminary examination, and, with the help of the lawyer, begin the legal business. I stated that my return to Paris would be soon. Most decidedly I discouraged any visit to St. Petersburg by her. The climate was awful—*grippe* reigned supreme, complicated with Asiatic cholera.

I covered the epistle to "Drexel, Harjes & Co., Paris."

Then I wrote Marguerite. I fully informed my

daughter of the local situation, directing her to send all her letters to me to the "legation;" also bidding her to write to her mother through me, so as to save one set of letters. I promised to visit her soon, and directed her not to come to St. Petersburg until requested. To have her at the Weletskys' would be awkward while her business was under daily discussion. To stay away from them would violate the usual Russian family hospitality; so she had better remain till I could join her. I cautioned her about writing any one but me, and promised, later, to bring her dear mother myself to visit her at Rjasan, as I felt no lady should go alone from Paris to St. Petersburg.

This was fairly well thought out for a man who shivered every time he heard the door open, or the working-girls give a giggle over their sewing in the next room.

A moment after Hélène joined me. "My robe for Madame Ignatief's ball will be a marvel!" she cried, then in a lower tone she asked me for the letters.

I gave them to her.

"Your hand is moist—you are nervous, you are fevered!" she said. "Now, go quietly to the hotel, or better still, to the club, and forget about this place. These letters will be delivered. I—I will be with you later. If you see him, tell Cousin

Sacha to call not earlier than five o'clock. I must have time to make a toilet before he arrives."

To this I sulkily assented. I got to the door and went down the steps, giving wary glances up and down the street, but the neighborhood was a quiet one.

No one was in sight save a boy flying a kite. Perhaps this was a signal! I quickened my steps; I breathed heavily; perspiration came out all over me, though it was a biting day.

Ah! it takes time to become a nonchalant criminal.

As I strode along, I meditated. I would be at least three days in St. Petersburg. I could not leave before that time. Surrounded by dangers, known and unknown, I must school my nerves; I must educate myself to become as cool-blooded as the Nihilist who could write philosophy while hand-ling a dynamite bomb. I must learn to chew up cipher despatches with my tobacco while conversing with the chief of police. I must——

A voice broke in upon my meditation.

"Ah! my friend, Colonel Lenox!"

Merciful powers! It was the chief of police himself.

Baron Friedrich stood before me. Fortunately my long steps had covered a mile or so of ground from the suspicious dressmaking parlors.

I was in a crowded street, where any sight-seer

might easily be. Acting up to my plan, I said politely: "Charmed to see you, Baron Friedrich," then looked at my watch, and continued: "You gave me the best breakfast in the world yesterday; permit me to tender you as good a lunch as can be got, to-day."

"Bravo!" he cried. "I can show you the best little restaurant in St. Petersburg. You might have remained here a month and never found it." Then, chatting on indifferent topics, he trotted along by my side, I cunningly imagining that my apparent desire for the company of the head of the Third Section would absolve me from all suspicion.

A few minutes' walk took us to the entrance of a place designated, *"Pichoir, Restaurant Français."*

"I admit," said I, looking at the narrow street, "that alone I should never have found this."

An impatient wave of Baron Friedrich's hand beckoned me in. We were soon seated at a little dingy table in a dingy private room. I noted with some interest that the potent head of the Third Section received no more attention here than ordinary customers.

The waiter disappeared with our order. I remarked: "They do not know you here."

"No," he said, with a grin. "But you, I perceive, have found me out," then went on: "I never eat at the same place twice in succession. Did little Friedrich have a regular restaurant," here he winked at me, "little Friedrich would be poisoned some day."

Having had no breakfast, I had been making a raid on the omnipresent French bread. At his ominous words, I dropped this like a shot.

"Ho! ho!" he chuckled. "Your appetite is gone, my poor friend."

I stammered I would brave very much for the pleasure of his company.

"Ah! then brave *this*," he answered, and fell to on the lunch, which had just made its appearance.

Encouraged by his confidence, I followed his example, and found the meal excellent.

During a pause between courses, he remarked: "My friend Lenox, you do not look well."

"No; I did not sleep much last night."

"Ah!"

"I was at the Yacht Club."

"And the result?"

I pulled out a handful of rouble bills.

"You were fortunate! And madame permits all-night dissipations? By the bye, how is madame? Charming, as usual?"

"No; shopping, as usual," said I.

"Ah! you are witty!"

"But truthful; she wishes a new robe for the Countess Ignatief's ball."

"Oh, ho! so soon in the swim!" cried Baron

9*

Friedrich, a longing look coming into his eyes. "Perhaps I will be there, also."

"Indeed?"

"Certainly; if the czar should conclude to honor the *fête.*" A restless, uneasy, almost hunted, look came into the little man's fat face.

"You do not look well yourself," said I.

"No!" he replied. "To be candid with you, the anxieties of my position are too great. I am like a boy keeping flies off the meat. There are too many flies. Some day, perhaps, I shall miss one, and then———"

"The meat will suffer," I interrupted.

"And, *mein Himmel,* the boy also!" he said, with a comical shrug of the shoulders; then went on pointedly. "You had an accident over in Washington to President Garfield—some few years ago."

"Yes," I replied; "he was murdered."

"H'sh! don't speak so brutally! What happened to the chief of police at Washington?"

"Nothing! I believe he retained his office," replied I.

"Nothing! Ah! it must be easy to be chief of police for you. You Americans are a great people. That could hardly happen here. It is either the criminal's head, or your own." He gave a little sigh, and then said briskly: "But I must be going. I have many things on my shoulders. I have not touched a bed since I arrived."

"Yes," I replied. "I believe I saw some of your work last night."

"Indeed!—where?" He was interrogation and suspicion at once. "What do you know of my work?"

In answer I related the incident that Boris and I had seen coming from the Yacht Club in the early morning.

"Yes," he cried, "I got one; but the great one —if I could only put my hands upon *her!*" A longing look came into his eyes, that seemed to sparkle through his blue glasses. "It would be half a dozen decorations for me, and the confidence of my master forever. Ah! but she is very cunning, very acute. She is a foeman worthy to Baron Friedrich. O-oh! I am afraid I shall never do it." Here he passed his hands through his hair in a comical kind of despair; then cried to me: "I have remained too long—*au revoir!*"

He had got to the door, when he suddenly returned to me and said: "You noticed no very beautiful woman on the train from Berlin to Eydtkuhnen?"

"Several," said I.

"Ah! yes; but one with dark hair, brown eyes, a peculiar fascination, and wondrous, winning manner; the graces of a child, the brain of a diplomat?"

"I did!" replied I, my heart in my mouth.

"Ah! you know her? Who is she?"

"My wife!" cried I, with a courage born of despair.

"Your wife! Oh, yes; ha, ha!" and he burst into a sort of laugh. "You are a *farceur,* you play with the chief of police. Americans will always have their little jokes." Then he winked at me and left me. Heavens, what did that wink portend? I felt that my situation was more desperate than ever.

The woman now sporting the name of Mrs. Lenox was so important to Baron Friedrich that all the sagacity of his long experience, all the astuteness and quickness of his Tartar mind mixed with the philosophy of his partly German nature, would be brought to bear upon her capture, because he felt that upon his success in this matter depended his own safety and career.

As this came home to me, I sprang up from the table, paid my bill hurriedly. That I must get out of Russia rapidly was the strong point in my mind.

To do this with some show of reason, it was necessary for me to undertake my daughter's affairs, upon which I had come into the cursed country, at once, and make some appearance of finishing them before I bolted.

I departed hurriedly for the office of the lawyer whose address had been given me at the American Legation.

———

## CHAPTER IX.

### SOCIETY FÊTES THE BRIDE.

"HERE he is! Just from the horrid lawyers, I suppose," greeted me in Hélène's voice as I entered my *salon* at the De l'Europe. Her tone was pleasant; her eyes, as they met mine, reassuring.

"Yes," I replied, "and I am happy to say things are going swimmingly."

"Let me present you to Madame Weletsky. She has been waiting half an hour, and telling me all about our dear Marguerite. Olga, this is my husband!"

An aristocratic lady, of dignified and charming demeanor, whose hair, now whitened by time, softened her beauty and added additional distinction to her manner, stood before me and gave me a smiling welcome; first by a cordial grasp of the hand, next by tendering a fair cheek to my salute.

"Constantine would have come with me, but unfortunately is detained at a meeting of the Council," she said. "However, I am charged as his envoy to insist upon your removal to our house. Your apartments are ready for you."

Here was another embarrassment. Under no circumstances would I permit Hélène to live under the roof of the Weletskys.

I was immediately assisted in this dilemma by the cause of it, who interjected: "I have already told Olga" (how free and easy she had got with my relatives' names!) "that our stay in St. Petersburg will be a very short one."

"A short one?" interrupted the hospitable Olga. "I am sure that my husband will not permit that." And she went off in her voluble Russian manner to tell us what a disappointment a brief stay by us in St. Petersburg would be to her husband, to her, to the whole family; crying out that we would not even see our daughter.

"Still, our present visit must be short, I regret," said I, "for as soon as I have arranged the preliminary details of Marguerite's affairs with the lawyer and your husband, business recalls me to Paris; but we will return in a month."

"How long will you remain now?"

"Perhaps not more than three days. Under these circumstances——"

"You could come to us for *two*," suggested Olga, insinuatingly.

"What! two *long* packings in two *short* days! Besides, if I attend the Countess Ignatief's ball, I have so much to do. A new ball-dress, and, unfortunately, I did not bring a maid with me, as I knew we should have to run back to Paris so very soon."

"Pshaw! I can lend you one of my women," suggested my hospitable relative.

Happily, this discussion was broken in upon by the arrival of the Princesses Palitzin.

"We have called," said the elder, who followed her card very rapidly into our apartment, "to make sure that you received the invitation of the Igna-tiefs' we mailed to you last night; and, furthermore, to be the first to ask you to come in our company."

"It is my office," cried Madame Weletsky, "to introduce my American relatives—my pleasure as well."

Upon this the ladies had a friendly fight over my "official wife," as to who should do to her the honors of St. Petersburg; Mademoiselle Dozia Pa-litzin enforcing her sister's persuasion by surreptitious pettings, embraces, and kisses that she lavished upon Hélène, with whom this young lady seemed to have fallen in love.

How long this amiable contest would have continued I do not know, but at this juncture in strolled Sacha, looking more handsome and more wicked than ever, apparently, this afternoon, having put some extra orders and decorations on his uniform for the conquest of Hélène.

"At last, my dear Laura," he cried, giving my

wife a too cousinly kiss; then paused, looking around,
and biting his lip at the sight of his *fiancée,* who
had suddenly and unguardedly cried out:

"Why, Sacha, I thought you told me you were to
be on duty all day!"

"Yes, but I dodged duty for half an hour. It
was necessary for me to welcome my relatives, my
dear Dozia," he said, nonchalantly; then, after a few
all-round speeches, led the young lady aside, apparently to make his peace; for as they passed me I
heard him mutter to his *fiancée:* "Why, she is a
grandmother—a grandmother, my little Dozia."

"Yes; but such a lovely grandmother," I caught
from the fair young Russian's lips in whisper.

During this *contretemps* the cards of several of
the Weletskys' relatives had been brought up to us,
as well as some of the Palitzins' friends we had met
at the station. The room was soon quite full of
handsome women and distinguished men, who had
called to present their respects to Colonel and
Madame Lenox. Among these my "official wife"
moved with a gracious ease that made her a favorite.
Our afternoon reception became almost a levee,
Hélène devoting herself to all, charming all, even
the American Secretary of Legation, who, having
heard of his countrywoman's success and beauty, had
called to, as he expressed it, "lay the American
eagle at her feet!"

Still throughout the afternoon it seemed as if Sacha was most often of all the gentlemen at my official wife's side, and to him her head was most frequently turned to receive his compliments in words or glances, for this young guardsman was lavishing both upon her, heedless of the pathetic glances of his young *fiancée,* whom he had left neglected in a corner.

A great deal of this time I spent at Madame Weletsky's side, discussing with her and the Princess Palitzin the disposal of our short time in the capital. To our remaining but two days more I noticed that Olga Weletsky now no longer objected, as she watched her handsome nephew at my wife's side. So it was arranged that we should dine at the Weletsky's that evening—a strictly family dinner; and in case we remained until the evening of the Ignatief's ball, that we should accompany the princess to that *fête.*

From this consultation I started up in astonishment.

There was a handsome piano in the room; Mademoiselle Dozia, tired of seeing the devotion of her affianced to another, had left her retirement and suggested to my wife that she sing for us. "You can't deny the gift," she cried; "I heard you trilling to yourself in the railroad carriage. I would like a little more of it!"

"You wish to hear my voice?" said Hélène, graciously. "Then listen—though I am a little out of practice. No, thank you; I sing without music, so I do not need a cavalier to turn over the leaves." This last remark was to Sacha, who had eagerly proffered his service.

The next minute, with the same touching sweetness that Nilsson used to throw into the old negro melody, "The Suwannee River" came floating to our ears. We all cried out for more, and this much-endowed young conspirator sang "Home, Sweet Home," without embellishment, but so touchingly, so pathetically, with so much of that divine sweetness with which Patti glorifies and ennobles this melody of all hearts, that after the last note had left the air we sat silent, hoping the sound would linger in our ears.

The song left tears in many eyes; in those of my Circe, who had conjured up the charm, and in the eyes of the reprobate Sacha himself, though they did not wash out the love-glances that he threw at the songstress; dew-drops were also in the blue eyes of Dozia Palitzin, as she gave a beseeching glance at this man whose carelessness of her love was making her young heart sad and heavy.

Our friends did not linger long after this. A chorus of enthusiastic plaudits for these American ballads so divinely sung, a hubbub of invitations

and compliments, and they were going—even Sacha.
It was dangerously near the dinner hour, and politeness compelled him to take his departure.  As he
passed out, Hélène was bidding her last lady caller
good-by.  I caught her words: "You must not forget
me in Paris, when you are there this winter—my
French address."  As she said this she produced an
elaborately monogrammed case and handed her guest
a card.

The lady bowed herself out, while I stood aghast
at the transaction.  The instant we were alone, I
whispered to Hélène: "You have betrayed yourself!"

"How?" she asked, nonchalantly.

"How?  By giving your card to this Russian
woman.  The minute she reads it your alias will be
discovered."

"Do you think there is danger in this?" she
laughed.  "Inspect my card case.  Behold my card!"
She held them up to me; I gazed astounded.  The
first was monogrammed "L. M. L.," my true wife's
initials; the second was:

---

*Mrs. Arthur B. Lenox,*

*No. 37 Boulevard Malesherbes.*

---

a duplicate of the *cartes de visite* my real spouse was using in Paris this very day.

"You see, I had them printed for my Russian tour before leaving. I believe in attending to details, eh, Arthur?" chirped the fair conspirator. I said nothing to this, being dumfounded at her forethought and astuteness.

A moment after, she cried out: "How do you like my American tunes?"

"You sing like a *prima donna,*" said I, in rapture; "but how did you know the songs of my native land?"

"I learned them for the *rôle* I am playing, that of Mrs. Arthur Bainbridge Lenox, *la belle Américaine,*" remarked this extraordinary creature. "Oh! I know half a dozen other negro melodies and the 'Star Spangled Banner.' Like to hear it?"

She threw herself at the piano and dashed off this patriotic melody, in a way which made me groan as I thought how much I would again like to be under its protecting folds and far away from the double eagle of Russia's imperial banner.

"Now I must talk to you," said I, "upon our private business."

"Well, what first?"

"First Sacha——"

"Not yet," she interrupted, looking at her watch. "I have only time to dress for Olga Weletsky's dinner-party." And she ran to her room, but stopped at the door, turned her head, and cried: "Rest easy! Everything has gone very well with me to-day. Now slip into your dress coat, Arthur, like a dear, nice husband!"

"A *loving* husband!" suggested I, at which she slammed her door; and I, thinking it well to take her advice, departed to my own room to array myself in my war clothes and adorn myself with my war paint.

An hour after this, we stood together on the English Quay. At our backs the beautiful Neva; in front of us the hospitable portals of the Weletsky mansion. As we entered these a blush of shame came upon my cheek—I was permitting the woman by my side to receive the honors due to my true wife, to accept the place of Marguerite's mother in the attentions and affections of her relatives.

But I was getting hardened and desperate now, and I gave a kind of reckless chuckle as I heard the lackey announce "Colonel and Madame Lenox," and we were shown into the state drawing-room.

Here we were met by the whole family, Constantine, Olga, Sacha, and Boris. These, with the two sons of Constantine, one a court page, the other an imperial cadet, and a sweet little girl aged nine, made up the family party.

This pretty fairy child, Sophie by name, was attended by a governess, a handsome young French-woman, who had a trim, lithe figure, and wore a rather *décolleté* dress, and was introduced as Mademoiselle Eugénie de Launay by our hostess.

Chatting with our host, I noticed that in some occult manner Hélène very shortly made herself mistress of the affections of nearly all in the room, especially of the little ones, the court page becoming *her* page for the evening, and the imperial cadet attempted his best military manner upon her; while little Sophie nestled in her lap and called her, much to her chagrin, "grandmamma."

"She is not your grandmamma," said Olga, laughing.

"She is the grandmamma of my little cousin, and she must be my grandmamma," cried the child; "my fairy grandmamma! That's what Sacha calls her! Sacha——" This was suddenly stopped by my wife's prompt kisses, in which it seemed to me she tried to hide some bright blushes and a slight confusion.

At this revelation of candid childhood, a little hush of sensation came upon the assemblage, broken only by Sacha's laugh and a sudden menacing flash from the eyes of the young Frenchwoman that I caught directed upon my spouse *pro tem.*

"Hush, my child," said Madame Weletsky; "your little tongue is too long for your years."

"Why, it's true!" cried Miss Sophie; "she does look like a fairy!" And she threw two admiring brown eyes upon Hélène, who, in some light, flowing gown, some creation of the genius of Worth or Pingat, looked all the little girl called her—even more.

"Be careful, or you will destroy the fairy garments," laughed Olga, for the child was nestling in Hélène's lap, regardless of the exquisite toilet she was crushing. "I think you had better retire."

"Till after dinner, mamma? May I not come in to the dessert?" pleaded the child, as Mademoiselle de Launay led her away. After passing through the door into the hall, I could see the young French-woman turn. Sacha was bending over Hélène, a Tartar love-glance in his eye. As she caught the picture, the governess's heart began to throb, and I saw a flash of something I could not define in her face; it seemed a mixture of agony and desperation.

"Ah—ha!" thought I; "Mr. Sacha is in the wholesale trade!" I gave a savage chuckle at this, as it suddenly occurred to me that my military friend was raiding my own ribbon counter, and attacking my fairest and most attractive line of goods.

Then the conversation became general.

I wandered about the old apartment, accompanied by Boris, who described to me the pictures that looked upon us from the walls of the room. This was a warrior who had fought in the old Tartar wars; here was a representative of the family who had enjoyed the dangerous honor of being Chamberlain to the great Catherine the Second.

As we moved about we came to the front windows of the apartment, which looked out upon the swiftly flowing river, covered with the commerce of all nations, enlivened by moving steam-launches, row-boats, and barges, that were speeding about in the moonlight.

"This will all cease soon; it is already late in the season," said Boris, with a sailor's eye. "Winter will soon be upon us; the Neva will become quiet, and on its ice will move sleighs instead of boats."

Then, looking across the silver tide flowing before us, I caught sight of some great granite buildings on the opposite bank. They gave me a start; I had read my guide-book, and knew I was gazing on that awful prison where so many lives have been groaned away in its damp dungeons under the river.

"The fortress of Peter and Paul," remarked Boris, following my glance.

"Ah! the political prison?"

"Yes," he said, and at his words a soft breath was on my cheek, a low sigh was at my ear.

It was Hélène, who said: "They are waiting for you to escort Madame Weletsky to the dining-room, I believe, Arthur."

"Ah! and you are the prize to the head of the house; but I sit on the other side of you," whispered Sacha, coming up at this moment to the lady.

As we marched along the hallway to the great dining-room, even Olga Weletsky's bright face and cheerful manner could hardly arouse me to my usually buoyant spirits. The sight of that great fort in whose underground dungeons so many political prisoners have died, where the daughter of the fair Elizabeth is said to have held up her manacled hands in despair, while the flood from the rising river drowned her; the place of present incarceration for those who offend Russia's czar—the place where I might spend the balance of my life— had proved a sudden damper to my wit and a crusher to my spirits. After a little the brilliantly lighted dining-room, and handsome table covered with flowers, for which the Russians rob what they call their winter gardens, or conservatories, with reckless prodigality, began to give me pleasanter thoughts. We had already, after the usual Muscovite custom, done good work on the *sacuska* of salt fish, caviare, and other dishes that are expected to make the appetite abnormal, and by the time we had run through a course or two of the main repast, the wine had been going around very freely, and under it I had entirely recovered my spirits.

Constantine at the head of the table was hos-

pitality itself, and Sacha, seated on the other side
of Hélène, seemed in an unusually happy mood; the
conversation soon became light, breezy, and en-
joyable, and toward the end of the meal I had set
the table in a roar by several anecdotes of my army
life on the plains, told in my best manner. These I
followed by my *pièce de résistance,* my celebrated
story of how Corporal Flaherty was captured by
five Sioux on the warpath. These savages, together
with their prisoner, had gone upon a fearful spree
by means of the whisky which the gallant corporal
always carried in his canteen in lieu of water; and
the gallant corporal had made his appearance at
dress-parade next morning, still drunk, but with five
scalps at his belt, of which he had deprived his red-
skin companions during the festivities of the preceding night. "I scalped 'em first and *waked* 'em
afterward," he announced to the commanding officer.

This story, told in my inimitable style, produced
shrieks of laughter; for my manner when I wish to
make a point is extremely humorous; in fact, the
Prince of Wales once said to me—but I digress.

Hélène led the mirth, so hilariously I thought
she would be overcome.

"Why," remarked Sacha, recovering himself, "his
wife laughs at his best story, and she must have
heard it a hundred times."

"A thousand, my dear cousin," murmured Hélène, with a shrug of her shoulders.

"Yes," said Madame Weletsky, "Marguerite has told me that story, and said that you always looked melancholy when papa began it."

"Ah! that is in private," said Hélène, with a *moue;* "in company I am always polite to my husband's stories. Eh, Arthur?" and she gave me a roguish smile, which set me chuckling to myself.

Upon this Madame Weletsky gave the signal, and the ladies left the dining-room, while we deserted men chatted together over our wine and cigars. Soon after, Boris, evidently divining that Constantine and I had private matters to talk about, and Sacha undoubtedly with a desire to be near my "official wife," at which I covertly gnashed my teeth, rose from the table and strolled after the ladies.

The head of the Weletskys and I *tête-à-tête,* very shortly fell to discussing the business that had brought me to Russia—that is, the settlement of the property that her husband had willed my daughter. A very few moments showed me there was no contest, that the Weletskys wished Marguerite to have everything the will gave her—even more; that all I had been called for was as a matter of form to act as guardian for my daughter's interests, so that no suspicion could come upon any arrangement that was made by her kind Russian relatives for Marguerite's future wealth, possessions, and status in society.

I told him that as soon as the preliminaries were all settled I was called back to Paris, but would return somewhat later in the season for the final signing of the papers. To this, Constantine, rather to my astonishment, made no objections; merely remarking that we would always be welcome to St. Petersburg. "You know that, my dear Lenox," he said, "both for Marguerite's sake and for your own."

Then he continued: "You will not think it impertinent if I, a resident of this capital, give to you, an American, who I am told, as a nation, are very free with their tongues, the advice to be guarded in all you say here. The police are very vigilant at present, especially against any one who is supposed to be politically opposed to the government."

"Why," said I, innocently, "is there anything new in the papers?"

"My dear colonel," remarked my host, with a curious smile, "the papers never know anything here; the secret police guard all." He lowered his voice and added: "Why, even my servants have doubtless some spies among them."

"What are they looking for?" queried I.

"Nihilists," he whispered; "always the same. It is the sword hanging over our heads." He gave a sigh and rose from the table.

As he did so the strains of the "Star Spangled Banner" came to us from the drawing-room, where Hélène was seated at the piano and again singing that tune, which brought the misery of helpless despair to my heart.

Stepping hurriedly in ahead of Constantine, I cried: "Don't sing that song! You know how it agitates me!"

At which Sacha, who was bending over the lady's shoulder, remarked, rather maliciously: "His national hymn agitates the American soldier. He is anxious to go on the warpath once more against his old enemies of the plains, the Indians."

I looked at him as if I would like to include him among the Indians, for his manner all through this evening had been growing more *empressé,* more attentive, more lover-like every moment to the lady who answered to the name of Madame Lenox.

The actions to the young guardsman had also apparently been noticed by Mademoiselle de Launay, the governess. This young lady had returned to the drawing-room with her charge, the pretty Sophie, and her glances indicated that for the same reason I hated Sacha, she was furious at Hélène.

Even Olga and her husband looked annoyed, for this reckless young libertine's freaks were too pointed to escape observation.

At this moment a brilliant plan for revenge came

into my head; one of these bright little thoughts that so often come into my mind to make me a joy to my friends and a terror to my enemies. Our party being a family one, permitted me a freedom that in a more formal assembly would not have been mine.

I strolled up to my official wife, and became the devoted, uxorious husband. I attended her footsteps wherever she went, and several times, as occasion permitted, tendered my wife the chaste salute of a doting Benedict, which from the very circumstances of the case she could neither refuse to accept nor omit to return. With diabolical ingenuity, I contrived that Sacha should see and writhe under the sight of these embraces, though I noted with some concern, astonishment, and wounded *esprit* that Hélène writhed under them also. But the party had become a very merry one by this time, and most of them laughed at the fervid nature of my attentions to my wife.

"Ah!" said Constantine, "you Americans are a peculiar people. You are proud of your affections and like to display them."

"Yes," cried Sacha, savagely; "they persecute their wives with love."

But the merry little dinner-party came to an end, as all things of this world do.

Olga and Hélène passed into the hall together,

the Russian claiming her for a round of afternoon
calls, receptions, etc., the next day; my enigma
promising the daylight hours to her hostess, but
saying she had given the evening to the Palitzins.

As we were going out I overheard Madame
Weletsky remark to Hélène: "Your husband is still
the lover."

"Yes," replied my official wife with a sneer; "he
always persecutes me like that after he has enjoyed
the champagne."

So coming down the steps of the hospitable mansion very glum and very furious, I placed my wife in
our carriage.

I had scarcely taken my seat beside her when
Sacha ran down the steps after us.

"Just to bid you a last adieu, my fair cousin," he
ejaculated, and shaking her hand, an unusual salute
for him, I noted with rage he slipped a little *billet
doux* into the fair fingers stretched eagerly out to him.

As we drove away, I said sternly: "Madame,
that note immediately!"

"What note?"

"The note that miserable *roué* handed to you."

"And you dare demand a letter addressed to me?
By what right?" she muttered.

"By the right of an injured husband," cried I.
"The right you gave me when you became 'my official wife.'   While you bear my name, I shall protect

its honor," said I, in an awful voice—"the honor of an official husband!"

My terrific manner conquered her.

"Take it, my protector!" she murmured, and handed me the *billet doux*, meek as a lamb.

A moment after she fell back, shrieking with merriment, upon the cushions of the carriage.

———

## CHAPTER X.

### NAUGHTY SACHA.

HER submission touched me. Putting the note of the reprobate Sacha away in my dress-coat pocket, I turned to my companion, who, recovering from her laughter, became cosey, confiding, and apparently dependent. Her state of mind appeared. to be impressionable. So I gave her a description of several of this young guardsman's wickednesses, extravagances, and infidelities, with perhaps some little embellishments of my own to make his enormities more patent to the lady at my side. "Besides, Hélène," I remarked, "this flirtation is an exceedingly dangerous one."

"Not to me!" said the lady, so nonchalantly that I was enraptured.

"For us both," I went on. "Did you notice Mademoiselle de Launay?"

"Oh, the governess," she replied, carelessly. "I hardly looked at her."

"But you should have. Sacha's wiles have evidently captured Mademoiselle Eugénie. She is enraged at his open desertion of her. She is desperately jealous of you. Jealousy in women produces sometimes the most astonishing results."

"What does it do in men?" returned Hélène, pointedly.

Disregarding this remark, which seemed uncalled for, I went on: "Our position is such that we can afford no enemies. The slightest suspicion upon us—the police will discover the false status under which we are living. Spies are everywhere. Actuated by jealousy, there is no telling what lies this Frenchwoman will fabricate about you. A malicious lie would injure you now as much as the truth, and in this regard women are perfectly reckless. Shall I tell you a story?"

She cuddled up to me and said anything from my lips was precious to her.

She evidently repented of her cruelty to me. I was in a happy mood as I gave her my little anecdote.

"It was in Cairo," I began, "where I first met O'Roony Bey, the Irish Mohammedan. "This gallant soldier had been on a steady spree for a year. There had been the dickens to pay in his harem. One of his odalisques, probably not having the handkerchief thrown to her sufficiently often, in a spasm of this horrid emotion, jealousy, had so lied about the rest of his wives, that, overcome by rage and the whiskey with which he tried to drown it, he had bow-stringed half of his harem. He was the saddest man I ever saw, as he sobbed to me, 'I have lost thirty wives within the year—*and no epidemic!*' At last the awful truth came out. I was in his palace when they took the lying jade out, tied up in a sack, and dropped her into the Nile."

"What extraordinary stories you *do* tell. Arthur, I am afraid you're a naughty boy!" whispered Hélène to me, with open eyes.

"I am!" I answered confidently, for I have noticed most women do not prefer saints as lovers.

"However, I shall remember your warning in regard to Mademoiselle de Launay, my own!" she said, as she made herself very sweet and cooing to me, at times even putting her soft arm about my neck and playing with the lapel of my dress-coat in a way that set the gallant heart under it beating rapturously.

I might have been surprised at her sudden change in manner had I not been accustomed to the peculiar freaks and emotions of womanhood, having made the fair sex my study—perhaps, I may say, my plaything.

Thus we reached the hotel, where a new surprise awaited me. In our parlor, at the De l'Europe, Hélène very sweetly suggested: "Let me help you off with your overcoat, my pet."

This she did in a playful, caressing way on which I did not place much thought; for she was always a loving wife to me—*before servants,* and there was a waiter in the room ready to receive her orders for a little tea *à la Russe,* a beverage to which she was much addicted, though I liked my night-cap a little stronger.

Receiving his orders, the menial retired.

"Now, Arthur," she cried, "hurry into your smoking-jacket while I make myself comfortable; in ten minutes we will meet here. Over our tea I have some good news for you—something that will be soothing to your nervous system!"

With this she disappeared into her dressing-room, while I, in gleeful mood, happy at her glances, delighted at her flatteries, strolled into my chamber on the other side of the *salon;* from which, in a few minutes, I sallied out, stepping into our parlor in a gorgeous smoking-gown and Egyptian fez.

A second after she entered, in the sweet simplicity of a tea-gown. It was a soft white robe that, clinging to her figure, would have made her statuesque had it not been modified by lace *ad infinitum,* that gave etherealness to the statue, and made it both coquettish and dainty—and to me maddening. The laces permitted glimpses of fairy arms and graceful neck; the embroidered petticoat allowed flashes of enchanting ankles and tiny feet in silken hose and little slippers. The sight of her drove away from my mind even the haunting fears of the last twenty-four hours, though her opening words called them back to me in vivid force.

As she sat down and poured out the tea, she whispered significantly: "I have completed my business to-day—*all of it.*"

I answered in excited joy: "You have made commun——"

"H'sh!" she said quickly. "As few words as possible on that subject."

"Then you are ready to leave Russia?" I asked eagerly, a wonderful sense of relief coming over me.

"Yes; as soon as you can get our passport."

"Very well," said I, my pulse beating more freely with the words. "To-morrow I can settle sufficient of Marguerite's business with the lawyers to make it reasonable for me to go back to Paris. To-morrow morning I will return our card *de séjour* to the authorities and obtain our passport to leave Russia; and the day after we will depart from this rat-trap." Then, a sudden joy coming to me, I took my official wife in my arms, and would have showered kisses upon her pretty lips, when she suddenly stopped, astonished, and horrified me with these words: "No more of that, my gallant colonel!"

"No more—of—what?" ejaculated I, scarce believing my ears, though my other senses should have assured me, for she had torn herself from my arms, and stood confronting me in a cold but haughty anger.

"No more kisses IN PRIVATE," she returned, a curious sneer upon her lips, which were pale, though her cheeks had each a flaming red spot. "It is *too late* for them now!"

"Too late!" I muttered. "What do you mean?"

"I mean *too late!*" she repeated. "Last evening I was at your mercy; I had not communicated the cipher and mode of transmission of letters to our order; for our cause I would have sacrificed—even myself," she sighed. "Now"—here her voice became haughty, bold, and triumphant—"now the communication is completed, my task is done, and rather than take one more unnecessary kiss from your lips I'll——"

"Do what?" I jeered, for her taunts and beauty had made me desperate, and I had seized upon her once more. "Do what?"

"THIS!" A cold circle of steel was on my forehead, her little buldog revolver was against my brow, her taper finger was upon its trigger. Surprise made me start back.

"Now," she said, "you know my sentiments; let us talk sensibly."

I could easily have wrested the weapon from her, but in the struggle it would probably have been dis-

charged, and in this crowded hotel have called attention to our rooms—perhaps have. caused police investigation, for carrying weapons without permit is
crime in Russian law.  Therefore I listened to her,
wracking my brain why this strange being, who had
been so kind to me the hour before, was now so
cruel.

"Let us understand each other," she continued.
"Till we are out of Russia, I presume, *in public,* for
my own safety I must permit you the endearments
of a husband."  This last with a grimace that indicated a reluctance that enraged me.  "But *in private,*
my dear colonel, please keep your distance.  We
leave St. Petersburg, I understand, the day after to-
morrow, so you will have only a short time to suffer."

"And you treat with contempt a man who is
risking his life for you?" I stammered out.

"You—you were very noble—last evening!" she
murmured.  "Be the same until the end.  I do not
love you; from now on, my lips are my own!"

"And Sacha's," I cried, wild with jealousy and
rage.

At this she turned very pale and muttered:
"Don't insult me!"

"Remember," I went on sternly, "while you bear
my name, while you are known as my wife, I shall
protect your honor—my honor, as if the nuptial
vows had passed between us at the altar!"

"If my wifely conduct does not suit you, my official spouse," she said, with a mocking smile, "you have your remedy."

"What!"

"The divorce court!" she laughed, and moved toward the door of her room, while I stood petrified at her assurance. "This scene wearies me," she went on, stifling a yawn. "I am fatigued—good night, Arthur." She paused at the threshold, then anger blazed up in her. Her cheeks grew red and flaming; she cried: "You took advantage of me at the Weletskys'; you pressed burning kisses on my lips that you could see writhed under your caresses. I could not protect myself then, because of our peculiar relationship—but I avenge myself *now!*"

"Yes—for the sake of Sacha!" I answered. "Because he suffered at seeing my caresses, you suffered also. You love this dandy major—this reprobate—this high-roller, the lady-killer of the Guards—this——"

With a mocking laugh she had flown into her room and locked her door in my face.

But the victory was not all hers, I reflected. I had this destroyer of my happiness' letter—I would read it. If it contained aught that a husband's eyes should not see, I would call him to account. He thought Hélène my wife—she bore my name. And disrespect to her was as much an insult to me as if she were my real spouse. I strode into my chamber, slipped my hand into the pocket of my dress-coat to seize upon Sacha's *billet doux*.

Desperation! it was gone. My siren's deft hands had regained the note as she had caressed me in the carriage—that was the reason of her temporary kindness.

I would have that letter. I flew back to the door of her room and paused astonished. Her voice came to me over the transom. She was singing the "Star Spangled Banner," and chuckling between verses.

"That letter!" I cried to her. "I will have that letter!"

"It is gone, dear; I destroyed it," came back to me.

"You have read it?"

"Certainly."

"Then I wish to see you!" I cried.

"To-morrow morning, my love! You had better go to sleep," she said. "Sleep will make you reasonable. I shall answer you no more this evening. Go to sleep. Good-night—once more!"

"Sleep!" How could I sleep, with the fury, the jealousy, the madness that was in my brain? I strode the floor of the room, muttering curses upon Sacha's head. The atmosphere of the place oppressed me. I put on my overcoat and bolted out of my apartment, then out of the hotel, and walked up and down the street. This woman for whom I had risked so much despised and taunted me. Every policeman that I passed reminded me of the dangers I had undergone, and was still undergoing, for her sake.

I walked the streets half an hour; then I thought I would go to the Yacht Club, but when nearly at its lighted portals, I paused.

There I would probably meet Sacha, and might do some wild thing, perhaps challenge him to a duel, which might bring about investigation that would be fatal to me; so I turned back.

Reaching the pavements of the Nevsky, which was still brilliantly illuminated, it not yet being midnight, the sign of a French drug store caught my eye.

Insensibility was better than the emotions that were tearing me to pieces. I stepped in. A young French chemist from across the counter asked me politely what he could do for me.

I said: "I am troubled with insomnia. I must have sleep! You can give me some preparation to produce that effect?"

"Of course," he replied. "I can arrange some powders for monsieur."

As he made up the preparation I fell to chatting with the man to drive away thought.

"How long will it take one of these to act?" I asked.

"Probably an hour."

"A long time. Can I not hasten its effect?"

"Certainly; take *two!*"

"How much will that reduce the time of action?"

"Probably to half an hour."

"And three?" said I, for I was anxious to get out of my mental misery.

"Three? Probably fifteen minutes, but three——"

"Might be dangerous!" I interrupted.

"Well, hardly," the young man said, consideringly; "but still I would not advise three."

"Ah! but in case of an overdose?" queried I, for I like to always know the tools with which I am working.

"Oh, take the usual antidotes for opium."

"What are they?"

"Coffee, unceasing exercise, and, if necessary, belladonna."

By this time he had made up the powders, which where eight in number, and handed them to me, remarking: "These will last you several evenings."

"Would you mind giving me some belladonna?"

"Certainly not, to a man of monsieur's apparent station!" He filled a little vial for me.

"How many drops of this for a dose?"

"Ten, and, if necessary, repeat it in an hour."

I paid him, and swallowed one of the powders before I left the store. Then I tramped back to the hotel, went to my solitary room, and finding that one did not act with sufficient speed, swallowed another. In bed the misery of my situation left me; pain gave place to insensibility, and I slept.

The next morning the sun was shining in upon me. I felt elated, almost happy, and feared neither the secret police nor the czar himself. The horrid grinding of a hand-organ coming in through the window seemed to me as beautiful as the music of Italian opera sung by the great singers of this world. Opium, what a fearful master, what a tender servant you are to suffering humanity!

I arose, dressed, and stepped into the parlor, to find a deserted table. Madame had already breakfasted and gone out, so the waiter informed me.

Not caring to see this being whose allurements, graces, and coldness had become to me a torture, I took a hurried cup of coffee and an underdone egg, cogitating to myself glumly that I would soon break the heart of the dashing Sacha by taking my official wife away from his wiles, soon be in the land of safety. I would move myself and dangerous charge out of St. Petersburg the next day, and as soon as across the German frontier—what?

That would depend.

With this project in my mind, I went immediately to the lawyer's, and spent nearly the whole day with him. The preliminary papers were already drawn up for the settlement of my daughter's estate. As her representative, I placed my signature upon them, and was ready, so far as her business was concerned, to leave St. Petersburg.

I strolled back to my hotel, to tell Hélène to pack her trunks. At the door of my parlor I surprised Mademoiselle de Launay. "Madame is not in. I called with a message from Madame Weletsky. She wishes the address of your wife's Paris milliner," she remarked, in answer to my inquiring glance.

"I will ask my wife to send it at once," replied I, "as we leave St. Petersburg to-morrow."

"To-morrow?" cried the governess, in a tone of relief.

"Certainly! Please present my compliments to Madame Weletsky and notify her of the fact," answered I.

"To-morrow!" muttered the Frenchwoman, as if this news was too good to be true, and she tripped away with sparkling eyes and buoyant step.

Hélène not being in, I stepped to the office of the hotel, delivered up my card *de séjour*, and asked them to send for passports for Colonel and Madame Lenox to leave Russia.

"Certainly!" said the *commisionnaire*. "You leave by what train?"

"The one P.M. to-morrow, direct for Berlin *via* Eydkuhnen."

"You are leaving sooner than you expected," said the man. "Monsieur has changed his mind." There was a grin on his face; he was looking at the main hallway of the building, through which, in most becoming carriage toilet, Hélène was passing, the handsome Sacha in full uniform bending his face down to hers, and speaking to her with both eyes and mouth at the same time.

The blush of shame came on me—even the hotel servants noted the flirtation of the lady who bore my name. This *commissionnaire,* this head baggage-smasher, thought in his ignoble way that I was leaving Russia hurriedly to take my wife from the presence of a man whose fascinations I found too potent for me to combat.

There was an awful look in my eyes as I stepped up to Hélène, seeing which that lady paused, biting her lip. Then her face changed, a smile played over it. She said: "Arthur, you naughty boy, you did not get up in time for breakfast this morning. I would have awakened you, but you were sleeping so soundly."

"Ha—ah! too much Yacht Club last night, eh,

my dear Lenox?" cried Sacha, with extended hand and cordial voice.

What wonderful actors these Slavs are! I knew he hated me. He should not excel me in diplomatic arts; and, though I loathed him, I seized his proffered fingers with a cordial grip, and answered: "No, Cousin Sacha. I never tempt the goddess of the card-table the evening after she has been very kind to me!" Next, thinking to give them both new pangs, I cried in my most doting manner: "You owe me my morning kiss, little wife. You won't mind it *in public.*" And knowing she could not well refuse me under the circumstances, I stepped up to my beautiful tormentor, and was about to salute her lips as fondly as ever bridegroom saluted bride.

But even in the act, so helpless, so hopeless, so pleading a look came into her wondrous eyes that I took pity, and my mustachios only brushed her fair forehead instead of lingering on the soft red lips that whispered to me, "Thank you!"

"I have just come from making my calls with Madame Weletsky," she said, giving me a grateful smile. "Cousin Sacha has kindly consented to take care of me as far as the Princess Palitzin's." She tossed him a confiding look that made me writhe, and continued: "You know I give the rest of my afternoon to her. You are expected to join us for dinner in the evening. *En route* I just stepped into the hotel for a heavier fur, the day has become so much colder; also to deliver a message to you from Constantine Weletsky.  He wishes to see you this afternoon."

"I was about going there," replied I.  "Having finished the preliminaries of our daughter's business, we are now ready to leave Russia."

"We depart?" she said eagerly.

"To-morrow at one o'clock," remarked I.

"You go—so soon?" sighed Sacha, a tone of startled regret in his voice.

"Ha, ha!" thought I, with a grin; "that doesn't please you much."  For I could see his mustache tremble with anxiety as he cried out: "The Ignatief's ball is to-morrow night; you will miss it—you would be its belle.  This must not be!"

"It is impossible that I remain," murmured Hélène, though she tried to palliate the refusal of her lips by the glance of her eyes.

"Yes," replied I; "madame is anxious for the delights of Paris once more."  Then I added an additional pang to my rival's woes; I said pointedly: "How delighted young Henri de Saint Germaine will be to see you again, *mia cara sposa*.  Au revoir till this evening."  And lifting my hat, would have departed, but a recollection of Mademoiselle de Launay's visit flashed through my brain.

I suddenly said: "I must whisper a few words

into your ear, my pet. Cousin Sacha will excuse you a moment."

She saw something in my face that made her respond to my request instantly. "Wait for me at the carriage, Alexander," she cried. "My husband's going to lecture me. It's about our trunks, as usual, I suppose?"

She put on a charming little pout, and the guardsman leaving us, she was at my side in an instant, whispering with serious face: "What is it?"

"Come to our apartments," answered I.

She followed me without a word. I led her to the door of her room. "Now," whispered I, "look your things over. Have they been examined?"

She made a short inspection, then said suddenly: "Yes, since I have been gone."

"You had nothing that might betray you?"

"Nothing," she answered; then noticing my anxiety, she whispered: "You need have no fears. Every article of my clothing I had properly marked before leaving Paris. See!" She held up a handful of delicate lingerie and lace, the sight of which made the blood fly about in me as I examined them, and found with a start that all bore the initials "L. M. L."— those of my true wife.

"No papers?" I questioned.

"No; all relating to that business I have in here." She gave her forehead a playful little tap.

"Ah! you are a deep one."

"I hope so," she said quietly; "but what made you suspect a search?"

"Only this," answered I; "I met Mademoiselle de Launay at the door of our apartment a few minutes ago. She informed me that she came with a message to you from Madame Weletsky. Five minutes after I see you and learn you have just come from the lady who sent the message. What need had she to send a communication to you that she could have made herself?" With this I gave her every detail of my interview with the governess, concluding: "You see your affair with Sacha, as I predicted, has made you another enemy."

"*Another* enemy?" she said, opening her eyes in surprise. "Have I any more?"

"You should have," said I, severely. "The young princess, Dozia Palitzin."

"Oh, she adores me!" she laughed.

"Also the man whose name you are playing with," I went on sternly; "the man to whose face your lightness brings the blush of shame."

"Oh, *you* don't hate me!" she said sweetly; then continued sadly: "Perhaps some day, when you know, you will forgive me. As to mademoiselle the spy, I shall take care of her." Next cried: "Both Sacha and Madame Palitzin will be waiting," and stepped into the hall, where, turning her head, she called back to me: "Don't fear, Arthur, my trunks will be ready for the one o'clock train." And so ran away from me, while I, with a sigh, took my route to Constantine Weletsky's mansion on the English Quai.

Here I found my Russian relative awaiting me. The preliminary papers had been sent him from my lawyers. These, after consultation with his attorney, he signed. A minute after we were together, and fell to chatting confidentially, he expressing to me his sorrow at our short visit, though not pressing me to remain. In fact, I could see it was with almost relief he heard that I was to take my wife so immediately from St. Petersburg.

Then we sauntered into the drawing-room together, where I found Madame Weletsky, little Sophie, and her governess, whose eyes again seemed joyous as I made my announcement of departure on the morrow. As I did so, I remarked to Olga that my wife would give her the address of her Paris milliner when she bade her adieu in person.

"Your wife's milliner?" repeated Madame Weletsky, surprised.

"Yes, madame; you remember you expressed a wish for it?" suddenly suggested the governess, whose cheeks had grown crimson at my question.

"Ah, yes; now you mention it, I believe I did."

"And, madame, I therefore took the liberty of inquiring for it," remarked Mademoiselle de Launay.

"She even walked as far as the hotel for it," said I.

"You are a good child, Eugénie," cried her mistress, with an approving nod.

"Yes," chimed in the little Sophie, anxious to say a word also. "Dear mademoiselle has been with us only two weeks, but she loves us all, even naughty Sacha."

"Hush, you mustn't speak of your cousin in that way," cried the mother.

"Who has been telling this child stories?" said the father, in an awful voice.

Under the silence that fell upon them all I took my leave, fully convinced now that the De Launay's visit to my wife's apartments was on her own account and for no errand of Madame Weletsky's. Any way, she had found nothing compromising, and I whistled as I walked along, glancing at the river panorama, where the vessels were taking in their last cargoes before the winter set its frosty hand upon the Neva and made it ice.

As I passed into the Admiralty Square I overtook Baron Friedrich. He gave me a pleasant smile and called out: "We shall have no more lunches together, my dear colonel; I hear you are to leave us to-morrow."

"Yes," I said, "but how did you learn that? I only sent in my ticket *de séjour* two hours ago."

"Oh!" he replied, "did you live here long enough, you'd find I know everything. I have to know everything. It is my salvation that I know everything." As he said this he trotted along by my side, taking two short jumps to each of my long military strides.

"You will return to us—later in the season?" he went on.

"Yes," I replied, "but at present business calls me to Paris," and would have given him some further reasons for my sudden departure.

But he interrupted me with a little chuckle and cried: "You have business in Paris—that is right, that is good! The naughty Sacha!" and held up a playful finger at me. Then saying, "My office is here," he disappeared into the great offices of the Interior Department, which front on a portion of this enormous square, while I with stern looks and blushing cheeks gazed after him, and thought of the shame that was being brought upon my name. "They think I am flying to save the honor of my wife. Curse Sacha," I groaned.

A moment after I reflected it was much safer for both me and the putative Mrs. Lenox that they imagined this the reason of my hurried departure.

Could that have entered my official wife's diplomatic brain—was she even more sagacious than I thought her? Notwithstanding this, Baron Friedrich's "naughty Sacha" and playful finger struck my heart with jealous madness.

———

## CHAPTER XI.

### THE POCKET IN THE BALL-DRESS.

I ENTERED my rooms at the hotel, to find three notes—the first a hurried scrawl from Hélène. It read:

"Hurry up, dear Arthur; I have already dressed and gone on alone to the princess's dinner; come after me as soon as possible, and save your reputation for politeness by being in time at the feast. WIFEY."

Under the circumstances it was just as well, I reflected, that she had driven to the Palitzins' alone. *Têtes-à-tête* with my official bride in her present state of haughty coolness were unpleasant to me.

The second was a note from Boris on board his ship at Cronstadt, inviting madame and myself to run down and inspect his vessel. He had evidently not yet heard of our intended departure.

The third was an envelope containing the passport of Colonel Arthur Lenox and wife to leave Russia *via* Eydtkuhnen.

Relief, happiness, elation came to me as I read the document. I could leave the dangers of dis-

covery and the tortures of jealousy by departing with
"my official wife" on the morrow. No suspicion
rested upon us; the rat-trap was open.

I dressed and went to the Palitzins' in excited
mood, to find there such a dinner-party as is never
seen outside the court circles of some great Euro-
pean capital; the gentlemen nearly all in gorgeous
uniforms—my coat being the only black one at the
table.

The company were mostly of the younger and
gayer set, Sacha seeming the liveliest *beau* in the
room. A new and wild joy seemed to be in the
eyes of this Tartar guardsman that took away my
appetite with a sudden terror and destroyed my conversation, and for the first half hour of the dinner-
party I fear I was rather commonplace.

But later the rich vintages served so lavishly got
into my circulation and I became my old jovial self,
keeping my part of the table laughing at my anecdotes of Turkey, Egypt, Spain, Mexico, and the
United States; in fact, distributing my humorous
stories over nearly the whole globe.

The only one who did not laugh at them was the
young Princess Dozia, whose soft eyes were turned
pathetically on Sacha as he devoted himself almost
openly to my official spouse, who sat upon his other
hand.

In Russia, however, no man is presumed in society to keep a strict eye upon his wife. I followed the custom and devoted myself to champagne and the various Russian beauties who came in my way, with results that might have been satisfactory had my stay in the capital been longer.

As it was I could not help thinking to myself every now and then: "This contest between jealousy and terror will be finished at one P.M. to-morrow." So, discounting the miseries and anxieties of the present by the delights and safety of the future, I contrived to make a tolerable evening of it, until the time came for us to take leave of our hostess.

"A most delightful dinner-party, my dear princess," murmured Hélène; "probably my last one in Russia."

"What do you mean?" said Madame Palitzin, opening her eyes.

"I presume," remarked I, "my wife refers to the fact that I have my passport in my pocket to leave St. Petersburg to-morrow."

"And take your wife with you! I will not permit it," cried the princess, hurriedly. "To-morrow evening is the Ignatief's ball in the *Salle de Noblesse;* it will be one of the sights of the winter. And, colonel, you will not deprive your wife of the *fête,* for—don't whisper it, either of you—the czar will be there in person, though it is at present a court secret. The emperor, for prudential reasons, never signifies his intentions of visiting any private entertainment until the day itself, but I think I can promise your wife a presentation to the czar. Why, it will be the event of her life!"

"The event of my life!" echoed Hélène, and through her came the sudden rush of some mighty emotion. Her form seemed to grow large, commanding, and noble; her eyes began to glow with a fire that I attributed to cursed female vanity and love of admiration.

"Nevertheless," replied I, shortly, "business calls me to Paris, and I always take my wife with me. I know American husbands are supposed to allow their ladies every liberty, but——"

"But she will coax you to relent by to-morrow," laughed my hostess. "Promise me you will, Madame Lenox."

"I will write—to you—to-morrow," replied my wife, slowly, almost falteringly.

"Oh! I know you will succeed."

"Not this time," said I, with a sternness that made the princess look at me twice, also at Sacha, who was approaching to have another of his "last words" with *la belle Américaine*. So, taking Hélène rapidly down-stairs, I put her in our carriage and drove off before that enterprising young officer had more than reached the curbstone.

This communication of the princess seemed to

have set my wife thinking; at all events, she said but little to me on our drive home, and I, being in very glum humor, for her eyes had not been turned once to me during the whole evening, merely escorted her to our rooms, and remarked sententiously: "You know I have the passports?"

"Y-e-s."

"For you and me to leave Russia?"

"Y-e-s."

"We depart on the one o'clock train. See that your baggage is ready."

"Y-e-s."

She seemed to sigh out these monosyllables as if she hardly heard my words.

"Very well," said I; "good-night."

"Good-night," she replied, and passed into her apartment, I noting that the gaslight seemed to make her look much paler than she did under the wax illuminations of the princess's dinner-table.

Then I went to the Yacht Club and put in two or three hours at baccarat, the fickle goddess of fortune turning her face from me so persistently that I got to grimly thinking to myself that I was in for a run of bad luck in other things as well as cards.

I strolled home in the early morning light, and reaching the office of the hotel, ordered them to call me at ten o'clock in the morning; that would give me three hours, plenty of time to pack my valise, get my breakfast, and take her who was my danger and my distraction to the train.

I knew I could not sleep in my present state of mind, so I took two powders, figuring that after six hours' sleep the call at ten o'clock would be sure to awaken me.

As I entered our *salon* to go to my room the light was still burning over Hélène's transom and I heard the sounds of her steps as she moved about. "Ah, ha!" chuckled I. "she has got more packing to do than I have, and has been making a night of it with her trunks."

Then I went to my room, slipped into bed, and the opium set my tired brain at rest. God bless those powders!

In my sleep I heard noises and had visions. I dreamt there was a rapping on my door and some-body said, "Ten o'clock;" that there was more noise and a voice cried to me, "it's eleven; look sharp, sir," and I cursed him with awful Turkish words; and then a sweeter dream came unto me: Hélène in some misty dress, with soft, repentant kiss and murmured farewells, and a dainty little note she pressed into my hand; and I was awakened by the knocking of the hall porter on my door.

"It is twelve o'clock, monsieur!"

"Twelve o'clock! I told you to call me at ten!"

"So I did, Barin, but couldn't awaken you. I

tried at eleven again, and madame, as she went out, said I was not to let you sleep a minute after twelve on any account."

"All right!" cried I, and sprang up eagerly and joyously to get away from St. Petersburg. I had just an hour to slip on my things, pack my valise, bolt my breakfast, and get to the train. Curse those powders!

Hélène was apparently already prepared for departure. But as I left the bed surprise greeted me —in my hand there was a crumpled paper and a hasty scrawl that read:

"Dear Arthur, I have decided to remain for the Ignatief's ball; the temptation was too great. So do not wait for me. Run on to Berlin to-day. *On no account wait for your*
HÉLÈNE."

I knew her handwriting, and stared at this astounding missive. I could not believe that for all the *fêtes* on earth she would take such tremendous risks.

I sat down in a dazed, undecided way and looked at my watch—in my hurry opening the cover opposite the face. "Blue eyes in Paris" were looking at me—the miniature of my true wife that in my four days' madness I had forgotten to look upon. It would be insanity for me to remain to face such peril for this lady, whom I glumly reflected could take better care of herself than I could of myself.

Thus resolved, I packed my valise in a very few minutes and stepped into the *salon* with it in my hand. My watch showed a quarter past twelve. I attacked the breakfast that had been waiting for me since ten o'clock—two gulps of cold coffee, a few bites of sodden toast and mutton cutlet, and I was provisioned.

The door of the rat-trap was open to me. I was passing out on my way to the office of the hotel, the railway, and freedom. I gave one look at the room of the absent Hélène. I was about to part from this being who had been my joy, my anxiety, my despair. I sighed as I thought what would be her fate, for no man could have endured her fascinations and failed to feel a pathetic interest in this modern Cleopatra.

But, choking down feeling, I was opening the door, when upon the threshold I caught sight of a little folded slip of paper, which had apparently been slipped under the door.

At such moments everything is anxiety—suspicion.

I seized this scrap of paper and hurriedly opened it. This stared me in the face:

"As you value your honor as a husband, do not let your wife remain alone in St. Petersburg, a prey to your rival."

It was in some disguised feminine hand.

As I read, the thought flashed through me that Hélène did not stay here for the Ignatief's ball but for Sacha's love. A moment's reflection and investigation confirmed my suspicion. I rang my bell, sent to the office, and ordered my bill made out. I also asked had any one inquired for us this morning.

No one.

Why had not Sacha called to bid her good-by? Why had Madame Palitzin not dropped in to say adieu?

They knew Hélène was not to depart. That was the reason. As this came home to me I suddenly became filled with the agony, the madness of a mighty jealousy. What, leave her to Sacha's love? Have that Tartar jackanapes triumph over me?

My risk in remaining I knew and appreciated, but reflected grimly, "If she could stand it, so could I. Her note mentioned my peril. She was trying to frighten me to leave the field open to the seductive Sacha and his love. But I would no more go than I would have deserted a military post given to my care. The honor of my name, my pride as a man demanded it, and the same dogged spirit rose up in me as in the Pyrenees in '74, when I held the little mountain pass for our master, Don Carlos, in company with Nuñez, the celebrated conspirator, contrabandist, and bandit, against a whole Spanish regiment; an exploit which gained for me the title of *A Cuchillo* Lenox—"To-the-knife Lenox"—all over Spain; or that other exploit of mine, when I, serving under Chinese Gordon in the Soudan, clung on to the little outpost near Berber against the whole power of El-Mahdi, and was the last man to leave the fort, a feat in war for which I was named by the fighting British officers "Bull-dog Lenox," a sobriquet that clings to me even now all over Egypt.

Thus determined, I chuckled: "I will play a little trick on you, my lady, and you, my lady's lover. You shall think I have left you a clear field."

I walked calmly to the office of the hotel, valise in hand, paid my bill, and told them my wife would remain for the Ignatief's ball. Then I stepped to the courtyard and looking at my watch, got into a carriage and directed the driver to the railway station, telling him he had *plenty* of time, for these Russian Jehus fly along the streets so recklessly I was afraid the fellow would get me to the depot before the one o'clock train ran out on its way to the Russian frontier, though he had only twenty minutes to do it in. Fortunately there was a slight flurry of snow, the first of the winter season, which made the streets slippery, and impeded the movements of the tough little Cossack horse; the whistle of the outgoing train shrieked in the air as I drove up to the depot. The door of the rat-trap was shut upon me for another twenty-four hours. I must confess to a little shudder at the thought of another day of this impending danger, this hand of Russian justice that might strike in a moment; this haunting terror that is more wracking to the nervous system than the wild danger of the battle charge, or the deadly rush of a forlorn hope.

But throwing this feeling of oppression off, for I had become partially case-hardened by this time, I chuckled to myself: "A surprise for you, Mr. Sacha; also for you, Madame Hélène!" The sudden reappearance of the injured husband!

To carry out my design, I cursed the man for driving too slowly, and ordered him to return to the hotel, where, thirty minutes afterward, I announced at the office my misfortune, and told the clerk laughingly that he would have another day of my company. Then I strode up to my *salon* to find my suspicions entirely correct.

As I opened the door with my pass-key, I thought I heard the sound of a kiss. I am not sure now. Perhaps I do the lady an injustice; but it seemed to me there was that sound in the air. I entered. The handsome Sacha sat there in his uniform, Hélène in a lovely tea-gown—but they sat *too* far apart. With a startled cry of surprise, my official wife rose up to meet me, a set look of horror on her face, which I ascribed to discomfiture.

She muttered: "You did not go, Arthur? My Heaven, you did not go?"

"No," said I, lightly; "I missed the train, but am not altogether sorry. My fair spouse, it gives me another day with you." And I gave her some husband's kisses that made them both writhe.

"Oh, this is delightful," said Sacha, with an ease of manner for which I envied and cursed him in the same breath. "My dear Lenox, you can now go with us to the ball. Madame's absence this morning was a little ruse of Madame Palitzin and myself," he bowed to me, "not to permit you to rob St. Petersburg society of the presence of the lady who will be the belle this evening."

"Ha—ah! it was a ruse," I said, "so you might go to the ball," giving my lady a knowing little wink.

"Of course! Here's the proof!" cried Hélène, with flaming face and eyes, that I attributed to anger. "My ball-dress, dear Arthur. It has just arrived!" She ran into her room, and throwing open the door, displayed a magnificent *toilette de bal.* "You see, since you caught us, I make confession to you."

To which Sacha added: "Yes, be prepared, my dear colonel, at ten o'clock. Do not fail to bring your wife. Madame has promised to dance the mazurka with me."

The effrontery of the Tartar made my face blaze with rage. I don't know what I would have said to him had the Princess Palitzin not intruded at this moment into the awkward interview.

She cried: "Colonel, I am delighted you remained. It will add another pleasure to the ball this evening. With your permission I will call for you and Madame Lenox at ten o'clock. I think I can promise you both *the* sight of your life."

Then the two ladies went into a whispered consultation in regard to certain mysteries of toilette and decoration, while Sacha, biting his handsome mustache in vexation at his interrupted *tête-à-tête*, took his leave. The Princess Palitzin, however, remained much longer. Hélène, seemingly fearful of a private interview with me, clung to her visitor all through this afternoon; sometimes apparently in feverish excitement, sometimes a despair upon her mobile face; at others laughing as if hysterically gay. Late in the afternoon the princess left us, remarking: "I must attend to my own duties now. I have a dress also to look after."

We were face to face and alone. She gave me one glance of anguish, and moaned: "My Heaven! why did you not fly as I wrote you?" then cried: "You would not go! Your fate is on your own head!" and passed into her bedroom, leaving her door open, while I walked up and down the floor, chewing the end of my cigar and thinking with internal chuckles how my unexpected return had

brought her despair—despair because I was still
there to protect my name and her honor from this
dashing guardsman, for whose love she would risk
her liberty—her life.

As I walked, I glanced into her room. To my
astonishment, this dainty lady, who had never plied
needle and thread before, was engaged in some al-
teration of her magnificent ball-dress.

"Ah!" said I, jeeringly, "it is not beautiful enough
yet for the eyes of Sacha? The bodice does not sit
becomingly enough, eh? Those white arms and snowy
shoulders will not be displayed effectively enough for
this Tartar's tempting."

"No," she said, with a submission that surprised
me; "it is the skirt," and went on sewing.

"The skirt—ho, ho! The train is not in proper
condition, the *panier* does not fit as closely as it
should around that little waist the guardsman's arm
will clasp in the mazurka."

"Yes," she said, quite docilely, for I had expected
a rise out of her on my last jeering allusion to her
lover. "It is the *panier*. Would you like to see it?
It is not convenient as it is arranged. There is no
pocket in it. I am making a pocket in the *panier*."

"A pocket in a ball-dress," laughed I. "You
would horrify Monsieur Worth. What is there to
carry? The cologne bottle, the handkerchief—these
are rather ornaments that should be displayed."

Then she astonished me more. She rose up and muttered: "For Heaven's sake, do not distract me! Let my thoughts be upon—" then checked herself suddenly and burst into tears, and cried: "In mercy —in pity to me, leave me to my conscience and my God!"

"Your conscience is pricking you," returned I. "Ah, ha! Naughty Sacha!" And quoting the words that had nearly broken my heart, left the room hurriedly, and went down to the Yacht Club, where I dined, and did not make my appearance until half an hour before ten o'clock, which would give me sufficient time to rearrange my toilette and watch over the lady who bore my name but was not taking proper care of it.

I entered the *salon* hurriedly *en route* to my bed-room. As I walked across the floor a sigh floated out to me from Hélène's apartment. The door was slightly ajar. The light shone through it into the *salon* not yet illuminated. Curiosity, passion, and the thousand-and-one conflicting emotions and miseries of my heart made me look in upon this being who tortured it.

Then I stepped back noiselessly, an inexplicable surprise within me, for, kneeling at the side of the bed, in her ball toilette, which was all pure, shimmering white, looking beautiful as an angel, with fair neck, shoulders, and arms uncovered and glistening in the light that shone upon them, Hélène was praying to the Deity as if beseeching mercy for a being that was already dead—a soul upon whom the gates of Hades were opening, a soul that was lost forever in this world and the next.

Not daring to intrude on such a scene, I passed quietly to my room, made my own arrangements for the ball, all the time pondering upon this new phase in her nature, and what it meant.

From this revery I was startled by a laughing voice in the parlor and a cry of "Arthur, hurry up, old man! The princess is here!" It was Hélène.

I entered to find both ladies waiting for my escort, and one, my official wife, more blooming, beautiful, and radiant than she had ever been before, ecstasy in her tread, brightness and triumph in her eye. Why did she pray as if in sight of death? Why did she laugh as if she saw heaven before her?

## CHAPTER XII.

### THE IGNATIEF BALL.

THERE was no time for philosophy now. I assisted the ladies to our carriage, which five minutes after was in the crush of equipages driving into the courtyard of the *Salle de Noblesse,* where the great ball given by Madame Ignatief, in honor of her brother named to the governorship of Western Siberia, was to be all that a brilliant nobility and imperial presence could make it.

"Look!" cried the princess to Hélène; "I told you true. The czar is to be here in person. See! the Cossacks of the Guard!"

I glanced out of the carriage window; about the entrance of the magnificent building devoted to the entertainments of the nobility was a line of Cossack Lanciers, Grenadiers in full uniform, and a score of footmen in the Ignatief liveries.

"You are sure he will be here?" asked Hélène, eagerly.

"He, the emperor? Certainly! Some of his chamberlains are already at the entrance, and his household troops are on guard; a sure sign of the imperial intention."

We were driving up to the great portals as this was said, and it struck me that electric lights always made Hélène look unusually pallid.

A moment after she swept up the marble staircase on my arm, Prince Palitzin himself being in waiting for his wife. Just as we reached the top of the great stairway I saw Baron Friedrich, and knew the princess was right. The czar was to be there in person. Following my glance, Hélène saw the chief of secret police, also.

Perhaps some sudden link in her nervous system (already overstrained) gave way, perchance some one jostled her in the crush, as the head of the Third Section smiled upon us, and murmured: "Ah! madame has changed her mind; the prospect of the ball postponed her departure."

Though she returned his smile and cried: "A woman would do anything to see such a *fête* as this," she staggered slightly and clung to my arm.

In doing so, the *panier* of her dress, the one in which she had made her own private pocket, swung around and struck me.

"Hélène," whispered I, laughingly, "that heavy smelling-bottle you are carrying with you will be a terror to your partners this evening."

"Oh!" she replied, recovering herself with an

effort, "Bouquet *à la* Jockey Club is not dangerous —often!"

But smelling-bottles did not occupy my thoughts long. The princess, with her husband, the Governor-General of Poland, led the way, and we moved up to the hostess of the evening. As we were presented, Madame Ignatief, with the gracious affability that had made her so popular both in London and Constantinople when her husband had been ambassador at those capitals, said a few words of welcome to the Americans so far from their native land.

We turned from her to give place to others, and standing on the dais on which she received, I looked over that great hall upon a scene of splendor the like of which I had never beheld, for a gorgeous magnificence that was more of the barbaric East than the civilized West, though it united the glories of both Asia and Europe.

To describe its general effect is possible; to enumerate its details, difficult as those of the kaleidoscope of beautiful but perpetual change. This *fête* of graceful women in the toilettes of Paris and the West, and gorgeous men whose uniforms run from the diplomatic costume of an envoy from Bolivia to the barbaric diamonds and Eastern robes of some of the conquered Turkoman khans.

Picture this mass of moving human color and effect in a room of superb grandeur and magnificence,

embellished by palms and growing plants that make
it a garden of Eastern beauty, and above all this
wave a thousand fluttering banners; illuminate this
scene by wax lights, numerous almost as the stars of
heaven; perfume and adorn it by flowers brought
here in myriads from the far-off sunny Crimea; throw
romance and poetry all about it by the delicious
music of the orchestra of the Grand Opera, broad-
ened and mellowed at times by the strains of the
military band of the Horse Guards. Add to this all
a motion, vivacity, and social *élan* peculiar to this
country of climaxes and impossibilities, and you have
a faint idea of how the Countess Ignatief's ball
looked to fighting Arthur Lenox, who had been more
accustomed to camps and bivouacs than balls and
boudoirs, though pretty well at home in either.

In the excitement, the intoxication of such a
scene, which stimulates every sense and every passion
by the friction of them all, can it be wondered that
I forgot the extraordinary danger and delicacy of my
situation, and even murmured to Hélène, who was
still upon my arm: "By the Lord Harry, I'm glad I
missed that train. I wouldn't have failed to see this
blow-out for anything."

"Are you?" she said gently Then a peculiar
look came into her face, and she muttered: "I hope
you'll enjoy the evening. But we must greet Constantine and Olga Weletsky. Here they are!" Then

she turned to my relatives and cried: "You are surprised at our presence.  You thought us *en route* for
Berlin!"

Upon which I greeted them also, explaining our
sudden change in plans.  As I spoke to them I
guessed they were not over-pleased at our lingering
in St. Petersburg, especially as Sacha at this moment
looked over Hélène's fair shoulder, and cried: "You
are mine for half a dozen dances, and last and not
least, the mazurka!"

This general claim to *la belle Américaine* was
now disputed by several other gentlemen, including
Boris, who had run up from Cronstadt for this *fête*
of the season.

So I let the wasps fight for my butterfly, taking
care that I took as a right the opening lanciers and
a waltz in which I flattered myself she should see
that I had not forgotten the days when I led the
german in the old mess-hall at the Point.  Does a
cadet ever forget his class dances, when youth makes
beauty's smile more beautiful, and adds romance to
military ardor?—for well he knows "None but the
brave shall win the fair."

These dances took place early in the evening,
and I am happy to say no one in that dazzling assemblage waltzed better than Colonel Lenox and his
official bride — for no jackanapes of the Imperial

Guard could surpass my dancing, barring their mazurka, which is a barbaric and national performance.

But though her step was perfect as to time, and her form floated in my arms as light as a fairy's poised upon a floweret, her manner was so preoccupied that, seeing my company was indifferent to her, I left Héléne to the devotions of any one — even Sacha; and with a silent imprecation on her indifference, determined to show her that other ladies were more susceptible to my charms.

So taking the arm of Boris, who chanced to pass at the moment, we strolled off together, this wholehearted young sailor making me promise that if by any chance we remained longer in St. Petersburg we would run down to Cronstadt, be his guests for the day, and inspect his vessel.

From his company I drifted into that of one of the ladies I had met at the dinner-party of the preceding evening, and we had a very merry dance together, but all this time I kept a husband's eye upon Hélène, and was tortured by the attentions I saw the persistent Sacha lavished upon her. In fact, this young Tartar was so pressing, so irrepressible, that he finally ran off most of his other rivals and had a pretty clear field to himself.

The conversation of two people beside me in the crowd of lookers-on showed they noticed it also.

A lady said to a gentleman: "That American

should look after his beautiful wife; with that reckless Sacha running after her there will be a scandal.
See that poor girl Dozia, his affianced, gazing at him
with pathetic eyes."

"Pooh!" replied her escort. "The Princess Palitzin
fears nothing for her sister. She even brought *la
belle Américaine* here."

"Oh! you men never see anything," laughed the
lady. "Madame Palitzin thinks Sacha a worthless
fellow and is anxious for her sister to know it also;
consequently a scandal would be to her liking."

"Ha—ah! and she imagines the beautiful American will do the business," cried the masculine voice.

This scrap of gossip, though it made me white
with rage, told me something I had been unable to
understand—viz.,—why a woman of the princess's
rank had so interested herself to detain my wife in
St. Petersburg.

Turning away from this unpleasing prospect, I
found myself beside Baron Friedrich. This gentleman looked fatter than ever in official uniform, and
seemed in all that glittering throng to be the only
one who had no friends. Alone and unnoticed, he
looked on the pageant of which he was no part
longingly and sadly.

Taking pity on his isolation, I spoke to him.
"Let's go and get a glass of champagne together," I
said.

"With delight," he replied, and brightened up. "One moment, however," and he turned to an officer, who apparently reported to him. "Now," he cried, "for the buffet."

Over our wine we became confidential. "You haven't danced this evening," I said, for want of a better remark.

"No, I am here on business, and I am glad my business will soon be over. Supper is at one—after that the grand mazurka. The imperial party will arrive to witness our national dance. When they leave I go home," he said, with a tired smile.

"The emperor comes late," I suggested.

"Always!" he said. "It gives time for the reports of all police and inspectors, guards and chamberlains to be returned. By that hour we *know* that no suspicious person is inside the outer cordon of troops."

His mannner was so confident that I grinned to myself. I knew he had no suspicion of Hélène.

A moment after, the music of the march announced supper. To this I took Madame Weletsky, Constantine bringing in Madame Palitzin.

As for Hélène, she seemed to wish to get away from us, and made one of a younger and gayer party, of which Sacha made himself the leader, drinking loving-cups with my "official bride," till I could see he made his uncle savage and nervous. Upon this the Princess Palitzin looked with a good-humored smile, though she could see poor Dozia's heart was breaking.

For her diplomatic gamble with my honor, I anathematized this great lady, but pitied her sister, and noticing she was not even engaged for the mazurka, though a charming dancer—every one considering, of course, that was the property of her *fiancé*—I claimed the honor of it, and received a quick assent.

The young lady had plenty of spirit, and now being convinced of her guardsman's flirtation, had made up her mind to have a pleasant half hour with the dashing American colonel.

So when the bugle call announced the formation of the glittering ring for this Russian national dance, I stepped into it with pretty Miss Dozia on my arm to do my *devoir*. I knew I could not cavort about in the wild grace peculiar to the Slav, but I would do my share of kicking, and in my present savage, reckless humor I didn't care much whether I trod fair toes to pulp, and put my martial heels through lace flounces and tulle skirts *ad libitum*.

Ah! the beauty of that dazzling circle! The ladies, all young, in court dress, *décolletées de rigueur*, with glittering arms, snowy bosoms, and shoulders that glistened under the wax taper lights; the gentlemen, most of them brilliant officers of the Garde, their uniforms showy, with high Hungarian boots, glittering spurs, gilded shoulder knots, epaulettes, and decorations.

Sacha conducted Hélène to the head of the dance, and I gazed in astonishment. Could she have the hardihood to take the place of leader in this affair where none but Russians, Hungarians, or Poles, who are to the manner born to it, can excel in its vivacious mazes?

However, my official bride seemed to have perfect confidence in herself, as she conversed nonchalantly with her cavalier.

A second after she grew suddenly pale. It was when the crash of the national hymn announced the Autocrat of all the Russias.

But as he entered, she grew haughty, commanding, and triumphant herself.

The ring of dancers opened to right and left, all present rising and bowing as the imposing form of Alexander the Third appeared. Stalwart, blond-bearded, and blue-eyed, he looked both soldier and ruler as he trod the floor of that ball-room, his sweet consort upon his arm, whose dark eyes I noted were anxious and nervous as they gazed about. Followed by his suite and bowing right and left, the ruler of ninety millions and his empress moved up to the head of the ball-room, and seated themselves on the dais, surrounded and flanked by the high officers of the court and ladies of honor.

Then came the merry bugle signal. Sacha led Hélène out; the mazurka was beginning.

This beautiful dance is a mixture of the cotillion and Virginia reel, its various figures graceful in their *abandon*. When danced with that devotion to Terpsichore peculiar to the Slavic race, it is a dream to look upon, an ecstasy to take part in.

As Sacha and my bride came down the room hand in hand, other couples followed them. Then to the sound of clicking heels keeping time to the wild national rhythm of the music, the whirl became wilder and more vivacious, and the *abandon* more ecstatic and madder than ever. Hungarian boots, spur-tipped heels, all mixed with rustling draperies and flying skirts of tulle and lace and gauze that floated from the waxen floor and showed as glistening ankles and as twinkling feet as ever set the heart of man to beating.

Into this wild revel I led the charming Dozia, to step my prettiest for the honor of "Uncle Sam."

Though I could not emulate the mighty Sacha, who danced like a wild Tartar of the steppes, I flattered myself I was doing very well, and was getting along swimmingly, when——

Suddenly poor Dozia gave out a little plaintive

cry and sobbed: "You are treading my feet to pieces, Colonel Lenox. Oh!—*oh!!*—OH!!!"

"Treading her feet to pieces?" I was doing more than that—I was dancing all over her! My two hundred pounds of brawn and muscle had become limp and helpless, and was staggering and reeling all over the poor little girl, and she was gasping and fainting under it.

In a turn of the dance I had caught the eye of my official wife, and there was a death chill upon my heart. My spinal column had lost its vital cord; my brain was a conglomerate of despair and horror; for now *I knew the reason of her stay for this ball.*

Her glance as it was turned on the czar was that of the hunter looking on his game, the wild beast gazing on its quarry! Fiends of despair! She had stayed in Russia so that, face to face with its autocrat, *she could do him to death!*

This had come to me like a lightning stroke with all its *proofs!* Hélène was willing to leave Russia last night. She heard that the czar would be here; it would be the opportunity of her life! Then she had stayed—not for love of Sacha, but hatred to the czar. The pocket in the dress was for the tiny bulldog revolver; with it SHE WOULD PISTOL THE AUTOCRAT OF NINETY MILLIONS TO DEATH HERE IN THE BALL-ROOM.

Somehow I got my partner to a seat, not greatly

noticed in the crush.   She was glad to let me go—
I was not a good partner.

Then these terrors came through me in flashes.
If Hélène did this thing, what would be the fate of
the Weletskys, who had introduced her to Russian
society?—Social damnation!   The Princess Palitzin,
who brought her to this ball?—Official ruin!   And
*my* fate—my *cruel* fate—I who had imported this
woman into Russia as my official wife, *under a false
passport, to do this deed*—I who had designedly
missed the train this very day?   Everything would
make me a *prima facie* accomplice before the fact.
*What did they do to the murderers of the czar?*

Eternal powers!   I might as well blow out the
imperial brains myself!   Cold perspiration came out
all over me.   My heart was beating at two hundred
a minute.   My brain was cold as ice, but delirious.

Into this hanky-panky of trepidation, horror, and
despair, one idea burned.   Something must be done
immediately to protect us all.—What?

If I told my friend Baron Friedrich everything,
would it save *me?*   It might—a *few* pangs.   I would
not be electrized; I might simply be hanged without
torture.   I turned my despairing eyes toward him.

Baron Friedrich was enjoying the mazurka through
his blue glasses.   It was a lovely but awful sight—
that woman with grace, abandon, poetry in her motion, and murder in her heart; for Hélène's dance

was like a swan's dying song, more beautiful because it was to be her last.

I half jostled my way to Baron Friedrich, to stammer in his ear, "For God's sake, arrest my wife at once!" but the thought that he would doubtless arrest me *also* made me pause.

A wild idea of taking her away with the authority of a husband came to me, but as I saw her I knew she would not come, unless dragged by force. Her eye when turned toward the imperial dais had the look of the hunter when he sees before him the mighty game he has tracked and ambushed for years —the shot of a lifetime.

I tried to think—if flashes of agony can be called reason. She would not have an opportunity of approaching the imperial party till after the dance. Then, when the emperor greeted his hostess, when the salutations were made, the princess had promised to present her. Even now, caught by her beauty, the czar was looking toward her and asking questions of his suite. When she stood bowing before her victim, she would give him death.

All this would take place very shortly. Before then I must act—if not—Baron Friedrich—I gave a shudder, then a sudden gasp. Nervously, convulsively, I had put my hand into my dress vest pocket —the one I always wore in the evening. It felt

four little packages. Powders!—*Opium!*—Insensibility!

Insensible, Hélène, under the plea of sickness,
could be carried out and taken home by me, her
husband.

I flew to one of the *buffets* and called for a glass
of champagne. Into it, unseen, I poured three powders, grimly reflecting that they would act quickly
on her delicate organization. In ten minutes she
would be harmless. Three might be dangerous, but
she did not care for her own life. Why should I?
I would take no chances in the matter.

Then, for the sake of appearances, I demanded
another glass of champagne, all the time fearing I
should hear the fatal report and be too late. With
these in my hand I entered the ball-room.

I gave a sigh of relief. She was still in the same
place, pausing by Sacha, exhausted by the dance.
There was no time to lose. This thing would not
last much longer. Already there were signs of
movement in the imperial party. I stepped near her.
She was panting. I tendered the goblet. Her lips
were parched by nervous tension. The fever of
martyrdom was in her veins. She seized the glass
from my hands, muttered "Thank you," and drank
it off as greedily as the wanderer on the desert does
the water of the oasis.

Perhaps there was something in the taste, for she

looked curiously at me as I laughed and said: "To your health, my dear wife! You have danced the mazurka better even than the Russians!" and tossed off the innocent goblet of champagne myself.

"Just one last turn!" cried Sacha, and led her into the whirl again with new grace, new *élan*, new enthusiasm! But shortly Hélène's movements appeared more languid. She seemed to dream as she danced, then fought to recover herself; and now, inspired with a new and potent force, conquered the drug within her for a moment, for the czar had risen. The moment for presentation was at hand. Perchance, also, the music gave her new fire, for it was that masked ball strain of Verdi's, that immortal dance music that has murder in it, which was now floating through the palms and orange-trees of this fairy *fête*.

She was fighting against some weakness, for she staggered and caught Sacha's arm, and he led her from the dance.

She began on his arm to move up nearer the czar. I saw by her look determination to conquer the languor creeping over her till she did her work.

She would wait for no presentation now.

I followed hurriedly after her, and whispered to Sacha: "My wife is ill. I know what to do with her."

She staggered back into my arms.

Then, like a flash, she drew herself up, made half a dozen steps, trying to force herself through the crush nearer to the emperor, and her hand went to the pocket of her *panier*.

But I was too quick for her; my grasp was on her wrist.

She struggled, and turned upon me one glance of despair for opportunity forever lost. One sighing moan—the drug conquered her will, and she went to sleep in my arms—within twenty feet of the autocrat she would have slain!

———

# BOOK III.

## DISSOLVING THE BONDS.

### CHAPTER XIII.

#### THE MASSAGE OF HATE.

THERE was a little flutter about us, and kindly women's lips murmured: "The beautiful American has fainted;" and willing masculine arms were outstretched to help me bear my lovely wife from the room.

But with the strength born of nervous tension I picked her up, all by myself, and disregarding the offers of assistance that Sacha almost forced upon me, I elbowed my way through the crush of uniforms and ball-dresses to a *buffet,* the one almost at the head of the grand staircase. Here Sacha whispered to me, with tears in his eyes—for these Muscovites are very impressionable—"My God! She is not dead? She exerted herself too much dancing. Such grace, such power, such *élan,* such beauty will never be seen on ball-room floor again!" and wrung his hands over her; while I, remembering the injunction of the chemist, called hastily to a waiter for coffee.

It was brought me, hot, strong, black, and potent, as it always is in this country, and forcing open her pearly teeth, that were convulsively clinched, I poured this down her throat, careless of the stains and splashes that dropped upon the white, shimmering silk and laces and gauze of her ball-dress, as she struggled in my arms.

As I did this, Baron Friedrich spoke in my ear: "My dear Lenox, is your wife very ill?"

"No," I replied. "This sometimes happens to her when she dances too much;" and looking at the fairy waist before me I libelled it, as I muttered: "She will lace herself so infernally tight!"

"Ah!" remarked Baron Friedrich, "grandmamma should not dance the mazurka so vigorously. What wonderful vigor at her age!" then went on: "The court physician will be here in a moment, by the czar's orders. I will bring him to you," and stepped away on his friendly errand.

No physician must see her! The trained medical eye would detect symptoms of opium. There might be an investigation. Suspicion meant ruin.

I hastily sent one attendant for madame's wraps, another to call my carriage.

Then carefully cloaking her, I took Hélène in

my arms, carried her down the marble stairs, stepped into my equipage, and grinned in the pursuing Sacha's face in triumph as I drove off.

This grin did not last long. As I slipped the tiny revolver, with its six little pellets intended for the czar, from Hélène's pocket to my own, the hoarse breathing of the opium sleep came to me from my charge. I seized her in my arms, and with kisses, caresses, and burning words, begged her to come back to life for my sake.

My Heaven, if I had given her an over-dose! If she never came to life! This meant police investigation, discovery, ruin!

As this flashed through me, I tossed my lovely patient about vigorously, for I knew that exercise— enforced, vivacious, and savage—was one of the remedies for the opium slumber; but she still slept on, her breath still came in long-drawn gasps.

In an instant, with one quick cut of my penknife, I had slashed the bodice of her robe from waist to shoulder, and cut the lacings of her corsage to give her air. Then heedless of her entrancing *déshabille,* I slapped her pretty arms and dimpled shoulders, and shook her till her teeth rattled like pearly castanets, and so got her to the hotel, the opium still holding sway over her.

Here being let in by a sleepy *dvornik,* I desperately carried her up-stairs, afraid to call medical aid; for what reason could I have given for administering a narcotic to my wife as she danced before the czar?

Then I let myself into my apartments silently and quietly with my latch-key—to get another sensation.

I had dropped Hélène upon the first chair I had come to in my *salon,* and was searching for a match, the room still dark, when suddenly I heard a light step upon the floor. Some one was stealing out of my apartments in the gloom, hoping to escape unperceived.

Under the circumstances I dared make no alarm, but still must know whether it was thief or spy.

I whisked out Hélène's revolver, strode to the door, and pinned the silent intruder by the throat, my pistol pressed against his forehead. "Now," whispered I, "light a candle or I will blow out your brains." I led the silent one to the table.

He obeyed me.

I staggered back, for I was gazing into the dark eyes of De Launay, the Weletsky's governess.

In times of intense excitement I am very cool. I stepped to the door, locked it, and pocketed the key. "Now," said I, promptly, "my wife is very sick. She over-exerted herself at the dance this evening. She has heart disease. First I will give her her medicine."

Then slipping into my chamber, I took the vial of belladonna and administered it as the chemist had directed. I noted a beneficial effect immediately; the pupils of Hélène's eyes expanded. "Now," I said to the Frenchwoman, "you must help me give her air and revive her circulation. Quick! get her into her bedroom at once. If you expect mercy from me, do as I bid you!"

My extraordinary calmness of manner overawed Mademoiselle Eugénie. She followed my instructions. While doing this I whispered to the De Launay: "You came here as a thief—a burglar!"

"No!" she cried indignantly.

"Ah," replied I, smilingly, "you can prove that—found in the dead of night in our apartments!"

For answer the Frenchwoman wrung her hands.

"Now," I said, "I can tell you what you are. You are a spy of the secret police. You need not be afraid to answer; she cannot hear you." I looked at Hélène, who was tottering between us, as we half supported, half carried her into her chamber.

"Yes," sighed the Frenchwoman.

"You are a spy of the police," I went on, "yet you dared to come here without Baron Friedrich's orders!" I said this confidently, for I knew no suspicion rested upon my wife or myself. "You came here on your own account?"

"Yes," she gasped; then suddenly and desperately

she cried out: "I came here for myself! I came here to find some letter for her"—she glared at our patient—"some token from the man who swears he loves me, to prove to him that he is lying to me; that, despite his words, he is infatuated with this beautiful American—your wife!"

"Now," I said, "we understand each other. As his mistress you wish to stop Sacha's attempted intrigue with my wife. As her husband I wish to defeat it also. Help me revive her, that I may carry her away from him as soon as she has strength to travel."

"Why should I aid you make my rival well?" whispered the Frenchwoman, savagely. "If she dies I am safer than if she lives."

"Because," said I, shortly, "if you do not do exactly as I say I will report you to the police as a thief—as a burglar. You obtained admission here as a government spy, otherwise the hotel would not have winked at your entering our apartments; but you had no orders from Baron Friedrich, and he will punish you for daring to use the name of his department for your own private ends."

I said this very firmly, as I knew she could have discovered nothing suspicious or incriminating in my wife's apartments or baggage.

My confidence frightened her. Mademoiselle

Eugénie shuddered, and whispered: "I will do as you order."

"Then," cried I, "keep this lady moving. Force vitality to her heart and circulation to her limbs! Massage her as if your own life depended upon it; slap her, shake her, force her to move about! A little roughness will do her good."

Encouraged by my orders, the Frenchwoman fell upon her rival, giving her a vindictive massage that would have astonished the most relentless torturer of a Turkish bath.

Her slaps were rough and sounding, and her shakings were so vigorous, so potential, that, under them, Hélène began to gasp and sigh and struggle, fighting with desperate resistance, and begging her to let her sleep—to let her rest—to give her mercy. Ah, what a beautiful sight it was—this massage of hate!—the struggles of the lovely victim, the silks and laces of her disordered ball-dress half falling from her enchanting figure, the rage and vigor of her rival, whose savage rage was giving to Hélène renewed life and reason.

During this, I stepped into the outer apartment, rang the bell, and, on its being answered, ordered some coffee made immediately, and sent up to the room, strong as possible. It was early morning now, and the domestics of the house ready for duty, so I very shortly received this; and returning to the bedroom noticed, with grim satisfaction, that Mademoiselle de Launay was still doing her duty—ferociously, and with good effects.

Then we poured the coffee down the patient's throat. Its effect was immediate. Hélène's eyes began to have sentiency in them, their pupils became more normal. One awful, reproachful look told me she knew what had happened.

My heavens, she was about to speak!

I desperately motioned the Frenchwoman from the apartment.

She hesitated.

I seized her by the shoulder and forced her across the parlor into my bedroom, where I locked the door on her. From there I knew she could not escape to hear any words that passed between myself and the woman whose last thought was that she would kill the czar, and whose first words would doubtless mention it.

I returned to Hélène; still the awful, reproachful glance was in her eyes. She staggered to me and muttered: "You miserable one! You have destroyed a country's chance of liberty."

"My dear," said I, "the *chance* of liberty involved the *certainty* of my death. I am not anxious to commit suicide."

"What does your ignoble life weigh against the freedom of ninety millions?" she whispered. A new and baneful light came into her eyes. She cried: "Oh, how I hate you!" then fell deathly sick.

I forced her to take more coffee, a little more of the belladonna, and then left her, for I knew she was sufficiently recovered to keep her tongue very quiet to all others about this affair, no matter what she might say to me.

I then unlocked the door of my bedroom, to behold the De Launay, frightened and drooping. She cried: "Let me go! I must go home now!"

"First, a few questions," said I, "and next a little compact between us."

"No! no! I cannot stay. If the Weletskys discover my absence I will lose my situation; for which I shall incur the displeasure of Baron Friedrich, who placed me there."

"Why did he place you at the Weletskys'?"

She hesitated.

"Answer!" cried I.

"It was at Madame Palitzin's request, I believe. She wished for evidence of Sacha's faithlessness to his *fiancée*. I watched him, and grew to love him: he is so fascinating, so winning, that—" She wrung her hands, and I interjected grimly:

"You could give Baron Friedrich all the evidence he wanted from your own experience."

To this she cried shortly: "Don't keep me! I cannot remain longer."

And I said: "First a little compact between us. If I permit you to go away without reporting to the police that you have broken into my rooms at *night*, you will notify me of any suspicious movement on the part of Sacha as directed against the honor of my wife?"

"Yes," she cried desperately; "for your sake as well as my own!"

Then I unlocked the door and let her go. I stepped back to Hélène's apartments, and found her still sick, with deadly nausea and gasping, but sensible and vindictive. I blessed this, for I knew that the power of the opium drug had been broken by the Frenchwoman's massage of hate.

## CHAPTER XIV.

### THE RAT-TRAP CLOSES.

THEN I sank down; the nervous, mental, and physical strain of this extraordinary night had exhausted me.

However, I am endowed with a wonderful whalebone elasticity of both muscle and brain. I swallowed a few brandies; took a cool sponge bath, and, making my toilet for the day, was ready for its embarrassments and dangers.

Over my breakfast I outlined my plan of action. It was simple—as soon as Hélène was well enough to travel, to take her out of Russia. I dared not go by myself. My wife's illness had been so public that for me to leave her now would produce general comment, perhaps suspicion.

I went in to look at my patient. She was sleeping, but her slumber was that of exhaustion, not of the opium-joint. As I looked on her pale beauty, I noted, with a sinking heart, she was certainly too ill to leave her bed this day. But on the morrow she must depart with me; nothing but madness could permit further stay.

I came out into my parlor to encounter numerous cards of inquiry and personal calls, all expressing their concern for the health of the lady whose beauty and grace had made such a sensation at the ball of the night before.

Among the first of these were Constantine and his wife. They had left the *fête* before the mazurka, and had only heard this morning of Madame Lenox's illness. With them also came the Princess Palitzin. To all visitors I answered that my wife was troubled with a slight but not dangerous affection of the heart. She had overexerted herself in the dance, but would be perfectly well by the morrow, when we purposed leaving St. Petersburg. At present she was too exhausted to see any one.

Present inquiries being answered, I stopped future ones by sending the above information to the office of the hotel, adding that we were at home to no one.

Then I got time to remember that every hour I stayed here added to my peril. Letters might arrive from my wife in Paris; my daughter might disregard my injunctions and innocently come to St. Petersburg to betray me.

I hurriedly went to the American Legation.

There I received a short note from Marguerite

reproaching me for not permitting her to come to
St. Petersburg while I was there, but said she would
obey my injunctions as telegraphed until she heard
from me by letter.

This disposed of any immediate chance of discovery. I went back to the hotel in easier mind.
As I passed through the office on my return I saw
Baron Friedrich. He cried: "I have been inquiring
after madame's health, my dear colonel, and am delighted to hear that she is so much better, though
not well enough for travel."

"No," I replied, "we go to-morrow."

"Direct to *Paris?*" he said, with a playful emphasis on the "Paris" that frightened me.

As I passed to my apartments I cogitated: "Could
he mean anything by that? Pshaw! It was only
my nerves!"

Then I threw myself on a sofa and went to
sleep. It was late in the afternoon, almost evening,
when I awoke. Delightful! Insensibility has given
me strength and destroyed eight hours of suspense.

How was my patient? I tapped on her door,
and received a low answer permitting my entrance.

"I am about to order dinner; you had better
join me, little girl!" said I, in a cheery voice.

To this she shook her head sadly.

"Think better of it!" cried I, assuming a lightness I did not feel, in order to raise her spirits.

"Official hubby will be lonely!" And would have patted her pale cheek, but she gave me a stab with her eyes and muttered: "You miserable!"

So I went to a solo dinner.

I was just contentedly finishing my dessert, for I am a man whose appetite it is difficult to disturb save by lack of provisions, when there came a rap upon the parlor door, and thinking it was the waiter, I cried: "Come in!"

To my chagrin Major Sacha Weletsky made his appearance. He cried out savagely: "I have called four times and have been told that madame could not see anybody. I am too anxious to remain outside your door." Then he broke out volubly: "How is she? She is better, I know; but has she recovered? Is she well enough to see one who is devoted to her both by relationship and by good-will?"

I was about answering that she was not, when to my astonishment Hélène's door opened and she came out, with trembling steps, but looking wonderfully fresh and charming in the *négligé* of an invalid. She said pointedly: "A friend's voice is so pleasant that I could not resist the temptation to come to it—my dear Sacha."

Before I could spring up from the table, my rival had got his arm about her and supported her tenderly and carefully to an arm-chair.

At this I determined to play the husband. "Very

well, Hélène," said I. "You can have ten minutes
with your cousin—but no more. Sacha can see you
are not strong enough to remain up any longer."
Then I amused myself with a newspaper. I don't
know what it contained; I only appeared to read it.

What they were saying I could not catch, for the
guardsman had drawn his chair very close to the
invalid's. Their conversation, however, seemed to
be pleasing to them, for when I looked at my watch
and cried, "Time's up!" I saw rebellion in the lady's
eye and rage in the gentleman's optics.

"As both your doctor and your husband, my dear,
I must insist," said I, blandly, for I knew I had them
both on the hip. Sacha could not object to my
tender solicitude for my wife's health, and Hélène
dared not tell him I was not her husband. So I
calmly got up, and despite pouts and entreaties on
her part and savage glances upon his, I almost by
force led Hélène from the room, saying tenderly,
"To-morrow morning, when you are stronger, my pet,
you may talk longer with Cousin Sacha."

Then I closed the door upon her and stood face
to face with my rival, who was pulling his mustachios
in a very surly manner.

"What a tyrant you are to your wife," he remarked.

"So would you be, my dear major, if you had as

handsome a spouse," said I. "You would look after her health carefully also."

Then I rang the bell and ordered some tea and toast for my invalid, whom I remarked was about to retire. So the usages of society compelled Sacha to take his leave, and I, throwing a Parthian glance at him, thought there was some advantage in being even an official husband. The refreshments having been brought to me, I took them in to my charge, who was reclining on a sofa, her ten minutes' conversation having exhausted her. She shook her head as I offered them to her.

"I insist," said I. "You need strength for tomorrow's travel."

Then a sudden fire came into her eyes, and indignation to her voice; she rose up and cried: "Of which your vile drug has robbed me!"

"That was to save my life."

"To save *his!*" she broke out—"he whom I had at my mercy; whom in another minute I would have struck a blow that would have given Russia perhaps freedom; a blow for the wronged, the oppressed, the down-trodden under the heel of this tyrant."

"My dear Hélène," said I, lightly, "you speak like a Pole or a Jewess!"

Then she astounded me, for she cried, "I AM BOTH!"

"What?" I gasped.

"Yes," she repeated. "A Pole—by my father's blood! A Jewess—by my mother's wrongs!"

Then she went on more calmly: "I do not wish to be misjudged even by you; you think I have the heart of a murderess. Listen to my justification!" And her face became sad, and her eyes pathetic, and her lips trembling as she whispered:

"My father was a Polish noble, one of the class which he whom I would have executed last night, and his ancestors, have been trying to destroy as they have destroyed my own native land—annihilated Poland. My mother was a Jewess, the daughter of a banker in Warsaw; despite the difference of rank and race, my father loved my mother well enough to marry her. For daring to mate with a despised Jewess, the Russian government, glad of the opportunity, ordered his name stricken from the list of Polish nobility, declared the marriage illegal, and made me, its offspring, illegitimate. Then came the uprising in '63 and '64. My father, maddened by his wrongs, fought in the insurgents' ranks, and when the patriot bands were crushed, my mother refused to give up the secret of his hiding-place. For this, my God! she—my mother, do you hear me, insensate American?—my own loved mother was condemned to the knout and banished to Siberia, though she never reached there; she killed herself rather than be a prey to the Cossacks on the route. Thank God, my father never heard the horrors done his loved one, for he was butchered in a burning village the day of my mother's scourging in the market-place at Warsaw. I see by your face it is hard to believe in such monstrous barbarity to a woman; but read the records of Poland in '63 and '64, and you will find such horrors were done not only to me and mine, but to a people.

"I was a baby at the time, and that saved me. My mother's relatives are rich. I was taken to America by an uncle; then returned to Austria, where I finished my education and heard the tale of my kindred who had been exterminated; and now, when my race is again oppressed, despoiled, and driven forth naked from their homes, why should I have mercy on him?"

"Because," said I, "Alexander is not personally responsible——"

"Not personally responsible?" she cried. "He is the head of the system! If you hear of a minister assassinated in Bulgaria, a prince kidnapped from Belgrade, an insurrection fomented in Afghanistan, though his own hand does it not, this potentate of Russia is the official head of the government that is its instigator. He has no mercy; why should he expect mercy? Your hand parried the arm of Justice

15 *

because you feared for your own ignoble life. For this I will never forgive you!"

"My Heaven, Hélène!" cried I, "do you hate me for the instincts of self-preservation?"

"Then you had better exert them to get us both out of Russia," she said, with a sneer in her voice; "for if the true facts of last night's ball are ever guessed, my fate will be as cruel as my poor mother's, only it will be secret—not public. The Russian Government has learned, from the horror of the civilized world, that private torment is equally potent, and better policy. Your fate, my gallant Arthur, will be equally——"

"You need not discuss my fate," I interrupted, with a shudder. "We leave to-morrow."

"Of course. You will find me ready. That is best for both of us. I shall have no other opportunity. Oh, if you had not stayed me!"

She wrung her hands despairingly, then sobbed:

"He would have been dead by this time; and I—". The fire of martyrdom beamed in her eyes.

She turned upon me, her eyes blazing contemptuous scorn, and cried: "Away! don't let me look on your face. You slave, who feared to die for liberty!"

When a woman gets into this peculiar mood of hysterical beatitudes, the best thing to do is to leave her to enjoy them alone.

I stepped from her presence and went out and

paced the streets; bought more powders, came home at midnight, took only one, this time directing them to call me at eight o'clock, and forgot my cares.

The next morning, early as I was, Hélène was at the breakfast-table before me—bright, chatty, beautiful. She seemed to have forgotten she was a conspirator, and exclaimed, "Look at my flowers!" pointing to a number of farewell offerings. Upon one of them I noticed Sacha's card.

"The poor fellow," she said, smiling, "begged to come and make his adieux at the station; but I feared our last meeting would affect him too greatly, so I forbade him."

I answered nothing to this, being busy in making our final preparations for departure. Hélène's trunks were nearly ready, and she accepted my assistance in the final locking and strapping. For even this day she was far from strong.

So at twelve o'clock, with thirty minutes to spare, we rattled off for the Warsaw station. Half an hour and we were in the crowds of carriages about it. The rush of people coming and going, all gave buoyancy to my spirits. I chuckled to myself that I had seen the last of Baron Friedrich, as I pushed my way to the ticket office and called upon the German clerk at the window for two tickets for Berlin, *via* Eydtkuhnen.

"Your passport number?" asked he, shortly, in the hurry of business.

"No. 7,287."

He looked at the list before him and rubbed his spectacles once or twice (every German in Russia seems to wear glasses), and replied: "There is some mistake, I fear. I have received orders not to issue tickets on passport No. 7,287."

"A-ah!" This was a gulp from me. Then I said desperately: "This passport, No. 7,287, was only issued two days ago. You must have made an error—7-2-8-7."

"That is the number. There is probably an error somewhere, but it will be impossible to issue on that passport until further orders. You had better apply at the Bureau of the Interior for correction of same.—NEXT!"

This was addressed to a German woman with two children, who came crowding immediately behind me.

Somehow I got back to Hélène without fainting; but there was a lump of ice in my breast where my heart had been, and my steps didn't seem to quite reach the tiled floor. She asked me no question. She only looked at my face, and hers grew white and pallid also.

"Come with me," she whispered. I drew her out of the crush, away from listening ears, and she said: "Speak low; we are probably already under espionage.  They refused you tickets on the passport?"

"Yes; what shall we do?"

"Act as if you are sure it is a mistake.  Go up and demand tickets again.  Stay, I'll do it for you."  She stepped up to the ticket office, and I could see she gave the German in charge a talking to that made him open his blue eyes.  Then she came back to me and whispered: "Send our baggage to the hotel.  We must conduct ourselves as if we were simply enraged at a foolish railroad blunder."

I ordered the baggage back, and, calling a carriage, said hoarsely, "The Hôtel de l'Europe."

Then I put her in, and we drove off.  After a moment I whispered: "You surely did not expect to get the tickets?"

"Of course not," said Hélène, lightly, though I could see that her little gloved hand was trembling.  "But I made every spy about that railway office think it was a mistake, and that we should have had them."

"You think it best we return to the hotel?" said I; for I had a wild idea that she would suddenly get out of the cab and bolt, with me or without me, for some nihilist haunt.

"Certainly.  Where else are we to go?  If we

are suspected—there are spies about us now—we could never escape from them by daylight. If not, the appearance of innocence is our trump card."

"You think, then, this refusal of tickets on our passport is a mistake?" asked I, a sudden hope making my heart jump.

Her answer made it lead again.

"No," she whispered, with luminous eyes that seemed to be seeing something that was indefinite but horrible, though her lips were firmer now: "I think the rat-trap is closed on us—that it means DEATH!" Then she muttered, "Forgive me, Arthur, for having ruined you," and fell sobbing into my arms.

But I did not seem to wish to kiss her any more. How passion disappears, when death lays its hand on you!

## CHAPTER XV.

### WHICH BROTHER?

WE were almost at the De l'Europe. She re-covered herself and said suddenly: "To play out our *rôles* we must appear happy, light-hearted, undis-mayed;" then smilingly bowed to an introduction of the Ignatief's ball, who passed us on the street.

We rolled into the courtyard of the hotel, and, taking my companion on my arm, I strolled up to the office and cried lightly, "You see you did not get rid of us so easily."

"Ah! you did not go?" said the clerk, laying down his pen.

"There was some careless error about our pass-port," replied I, "which may detain us a day or two. Perhaps it is better, after all, for my wife is hardly strong enough to travel. We will occupy the same suite of apartments."

At this the man answered suspiciously: "It will be necessary to see the secretary," so I followed him to that functionary's private office, and ex-plained matters.

To my astonishment, that gentleman, who had been obsequiously polite to us before, appeared worried and dismayed, and said: "Colonel Lenox, you will pardon me for speaking plainly. It is impossible for us to receive any one whose passport is defective. The rules of the police forbid that."

"Defective?" cried I, forcing myself to indignation; "do you call that passport defective? If you do, I will send for my friend, Baron Friedrich. His guarantee, I presume, will be sufficient?"

"Perfectly," murmured the official. "You will excuse me for making any difficulty, but our orders from the police department are imperative."

He called a boy, and by him I sent two lines to my all-powerful friend, simply asking him to come up to the De l'Europe to see me for a moment, as soon as possible.

Then I returned to Hélène. She took my arm, and I told her what had happened. She whispered:

"When you sent for Baron Friedrich you did a very wise thing. It will show him that we consider ourselves above all doubt."

Within half an hour Baron Friedrich came dashing in, and smiled an inscrutable smile at us through his blue eye-glasses.

"Ah! my dear Lenox," he cried effusively; "and madame—she was not well enough to leave this afternoon?" and opened his eyes in astonishment, I thought a little too wide, when I told him of tickets being refused on our passports.

"Ah! some mistake of those beastly railway clerks. Passports pass through half a dozen hands, and an error by any one destroys the whole routine. My dear Lenox, have no uneasiness; a day or two for red-tape and all will be arranged. Take good care of your beautiful wife. It is, perhaps, better that she does not travel immediately."

"But," laughed Hélène, with a *petite moue*, "they won't let us into our apartments on this passport without your guaranteeing it."

"What!" he cried, indignation filling his fat little frame as he strode to the secretary, who cringed before him, and gave him such a rating as I have never heard outside Russia or Turkey, where men treat those below them as brutes.

"Take good care of my friends," he cried, "you dog of a hotel-man; take *very* good care of my friends; the best in the house for them!" Then he turned to us, and murmured: "And now, my dear Lenox, I am busy. You will enjoy a day or two more in St. Petersburg. Take your wife to the opera; be happy to-night; *bon jour!*" He bade us an effusive farewell, kissing Hélène's gloved hand several times, and departed.

We were shown back by obsequious lackeys to

our apartments, and our baggage being arranged, and ourselves alone, I whispered to Hélène: "Do you think he suspects us?"

"I fear so," replied Hélène. "He appeared too much surprised." Then she whispered suddenly to me: "Can you think of anything that could have made him doubt me?"

I said, "No," but now thought it best to inform her of my curious meeting with Mademoiselle de Launay after the ball.

"I don't think that had anything to do with it," she replied. "That young lady is simply jealous of Sacha. And you are jealous of him also—jealous of a Russian?" And she commenced to laugh; then said pointedly: "Perhaps I shall have use for Mademoiselle Eugénie at the last," and busied herself unpacking.

Half an hour after we were broken in upon by Sacha and the Princess Palitzin.

"I went to the train to bid you adieu," replied the major; "and heard you were not going—bless God for His mercies."

"And so," interrupted Madame Palitzin, "we have come to ask you to go with us to the Michael Theatre this evening. Amusement will be good for both of you; neither of you look over-happy!"

"No," said I; "playing nurse does not agree with me."

"And the *rôle* of invalid is not my *forte*," smiled
Hélène.

"So it is settled, you come; I will take no refusal
from my cousins!" cried Sacha.

To this I agreed, for anything was better than
this waiting—waiting—waiting for the hand to fall.

Then they went away; and I would have been
almost happy now had my nerves permitted it, in a
wild, nasty, wicked way; for Hélène, who had been
so cool to me two days before, and spurned me, and
told me she hated me last night, was now softly
pathetic, every now and then coming to me and
begging me to forgive her for having destroyed my
life—though such requests were not calming to
my nervous system, and I shuddered as I forgave
her.

"I will go to the legation and see if there are
any letters," I said; for I felt under the circumstances
anything was better than inaction. "I will return in
time to take you to the theatre."

As I was about to step out she called me back
to her and whispered: "That revolver you deprived
me of the other night."

I handed it silently to her. Her eyes answered
my question. She did not mean to be taken alive.

Then I went to the legation. No letters from
my wife. This was curious. I should have had one

by this time. Then to the Yacht Club, where among others I met Boris Weletsky. We dined together. Over dinner, in answer to his questions, I told him I should remain a day or two longer in St. Petersburg. My wife was hardly yet strong enough to travel.

"Very well," cried this hospitable young fellow, "then I hold you to your promise. Bring madame down to Cronstadt to-morrow, inspect my ship and the forts. Be my guest."

I could hardly answer his question without consulting Hélène, and told him so.

"All right. After the theatre meet me here and let me know," he said.

I promised to do this, and went straight to the hotel. Hélène was already dressed for the theatre, a slight trace of color on her cheeks, that I thought was not natural, for the first time.

I breathlessly asked: "What has happened?"

"Since you were away? Nothing! It is always this way till the blow is struck. The more silent the secret police, the more deadly. Between ourselves," she said, with a slight smile, "I think Baron Friedrich is waiting for something—some final proof—before he dares to put his hand upon us."

Then I told her of Weletsky's invitation.

"What do you say to it?" I asked. "We might as well enjoy our privileges while they last."

"Slip on your dress-suit and I will consider and answer you."

I went into the next room, and while engaged in my toilet heard a little cry from Hélène. It seemed to be of joy. I took a peep at her. She was reading the Russian papers apparently, as I thought at the time examining the shipping list.

When I entered, ready for the theatre, a new hope seemed to be in her eyes. She put her hand confidingly on my arm to walk down to the carriage.

I said: "Have you determined about this invitation to visit Cronstadt?"

"Yes," she answered. "Accept it at once. Let us go down on an early morning boat."

Ten minutes after this we were gazing from one of the boxes of the main tier upon the performance of "Giroflé and Girofla" by a dashing French company just from Paris, the prima donna of which was making an enormous hit, as is usual in Russia, where everything is a grand *coup* or a great failure. The face of this artiste appeared familiar to me.

Here we were shortly joined by Madame Palitzin, attended by the ubiquitous Sacha. He had two lovely bouquets in his hand, and after the generous manner of the Russian race, tendered one of pale *La France* roses to the princess, the other, of some

pure white flowers and buds, to my wife. Hélène
bent over this a little curiously, I thought, and fierce
fires of jealousy swept through me, for I saw there
was a letter concealed in the blossoms.

As I noted this, the theatre resounded with applause upon the waltz song of Giroflé. "She shall
never read it!" I thought, and with an instinct born
of the moment, I threw myself heart and soul into
the ovation to the singer. I led the applause, and
bravoed stronger and wilder than the most enthusiastic
Muscovite in the building. Then, as if carried away
by uncontrollable admiration, I seized the bouquet
from my wife's lap, and hurled it at the feet of the
*diva* on the stage. Then I suddenly came to myself, and bowed my humble apologies to Hélène,
whose eyes shot fiery glances upon me, though they
were not half as savage as those with which the
major of the *Chevalier Garde* favored me from the
rear of the box.

A few seconds after, while Sacha was occupied
with the princess in some private conversation,
Hélène whispered to me: "Get that bouquet back.
It had a note in it."

"His *billet-doux*," returned I. "Never!"

Upon which her face grew very pale, and she
whispered to me again: "Get the note back into my
hands, as you value your safety!" Her eyes told me
she meant what she said.

After a moment I excused myself to our party, and sauntered out of the theatre, trying to think how to do the trick. I put my thoughts upon the prima donna, and remembered at last that she had been a little actress who was once quite friendly with me, when she sang at the *Varieties,* in my earlier Parisian days. I looked at my programme, and found I was not mistaken.

Strolling around to the stage entrance, I sent in my card to Mlle. Eulalie de Bonbon. How aristocratic most French actresses are! Their stage names always have a "de" in them.

Answer was very shortly brought me, and I was shown up to this young lady, who said: "My dear Colonel Lenox, I can give you only a moment. You were charming to remember me."

"I threw you a bouquet," I said.

"Ah, yes, as a reminiscence of dear old times— you naughty boy!"

"That bouquet has a note in it *not* addressed to you."

"Ah, *not* for me! *Diable!* Then whom was it for?" she cried, anger coming into her eyes. "Was it for the miserable Seraphine, who cannot dance, or that audacious Georgette, who attempts to sing with me, but can only croak?"

"No," I replied; "the note was for my wife. I stole the bouquet from her. You can keep the flowers, Eulalie; it's the note I want."

"For revenge?" she cried, laughing. "Ha—ah, a duel, *mon brave!*"

"I hardly think so," I said. "I leave St. Petersburg in a day or two."

"Ah! Very well! I shall be at the *Varieties* again this winter. You can throw me more bouquets. Adieu!" As she handed me the note, the address caught her eye. She kissed her hand to me, cried, "Madame has been naughty, eh?" then laughed: "That *diable* Sacha!" and grinned at me in a way that made me want to wring her neck, as she skipped off to her cue of entrance.

I looked at the missive.

Should I read it? Yes! Hélène said my safety depended upon it. I inspected it by the light of an electric lamp in the street. Its contents mystified me. It only contained four words:

"Seven o'clock to-morrow evening."

I strolled back to our box, and as we journeyed home from the performance, handed it to Hélène. She opened it, glanced at it, gave a sigh of relief, said, "Very good"—nothing more.

At the door of our apartments she turned and remarked to me: "I don't think you are very good company, my dear Arthur. Stroll down to the Yacht Club and tell Boris we will be his guests. Make a night of it there." I saw she wanted to get rid of me.

"And you?" I said.

"The less you know of my movements, the better for your safety now," she whispered.

I walked to the Yacht Club and delighted Boris by arranging that we should go down with him on the early boat for Cronstadt.

Then I tried to play baccarat, but I couldn't keep my thoughts on the game. The clubs all looked like policemen's clubs, and the grinning knaves all grinned like Baron Friedrich.

I gave it up, walked homeward, and entered my apartments to find Hélène—NOT THERE!

I tried to wait for her. The suspense was too long and too terrible. Every moment I expected to hear the rap on the door, and the "Open in the name of the czar!" The porter, as he collected the boots, nearly made my heart jump out of my mouth.

I took two powders. They lulled me to sleep. God bless the poppy!

Hélène's voice awakened me. The autumn sun

was in the room. I sprang up with a yell, at which she laughed and said: "No; not yet! We have another day, perhaps. Let's make the best use of it. Nine o'clock, Arthur! Up and catch the Cronstadt boat."

She hurried through breakfast. I did not eat. Somehow my appetite was getting bad. Then we drove to the quay, boarded the steamboat, and in company with Boris, who had awaited us, darted out upon the swift blue Neva down past picturesque islands dotted with villas and small palaces. Peterhof to the left displayed its clustered marble columns and gilded domes as we ran out into the Gulf of Finland.

Cronstadt's granite forts and fleet at mooring could be faintly descried; behind us St. Petersburg, dominated by the great cross on the giant dome of St. Isaac's, which hovered with its mute benediction over a helpless people.

An hour afterward we landed at the granite pier of Cronstadt, took an early lunch at the *Hôtel de Russie*, and were soon on board the *Vsadnik*, Boris welcoming us as her captain. On this fleet despatch boat we glided over the glassy waters of the gulf and visited several of the huge iron-clads and outer forts, my companion chatting vivaciously with the young Russian officer.

"All the vessels are stopped before the forts, I believe," said she, with an inquiring smile.

"Oh, yes! Incoming craft await a pilot; outgoing vessels slow down till inspected, and wait till the conclusion of passport examination. Every vessel's name and clearance is telegraphed here; she shows her flag and number on slowing down."

"And you have the boarding duty to-day? It will be quite interesting for us to see this work," murmured Hélène. "I suppose we can go on board some of them."

"Certainly," said the gallant Weletsky. "Any one you wish."

As he spoke, several columns of smoke showed in the distance that outgoing steamers were approaching from St. Petersburg. The forts began to signal to our vessel. Weletsky's under officer approached and reported. The young commander gave his orders for the boarding parties.

As the vessels neared us, several boats were lowered and the *Vsadnik* stood along under steerage way. One or two of the coasting steamers were nearing us. These slowed up. Our boats boarded and examined them and took off the customs inspectors. A large sea-going steamer followed immediately after these smaller fry.

"What vessel is that?" asked Hélène, languidly. "Yes—the big one—the one with the two funnels."

"The Swedish steamer *Dalecarlia*, outward bound," was the reply.

"She is very beautiful," said my wife.

"You would like to see her?" inquired Boris.

"Yes, she will do as well as another. She is stopping now."

"Very well; we will go! You shall see the routine of examination on her!" cried our host.

His barge was waiting him. He gallantly escorted my wife down the gangway to it. I followed after. As we neared this splendid steamer, her side gangway was quickly lowered. The Russian flag in our boat indicated a commanding officer, and the merchant captain, hat in hand, was at the companionway.

Weletsky knew him from his continued passing, and presented him to us as Captain Olafson, of Stockholm. He immediately offered his arm to Hélène, and showed us the steamer. Boris excused himself to us, and proceeded to his duties, examined the passenger lists, checked off the passports, and looked over the custom-house papers.

While this was going on, I saw something that astonished me. Unnoticed by any one but me, for the decks were crowded with passengers and the hurry and bustle of departure were going on, Hélène and the Swedish captain were conversing hurriedly, excitedly.

Boris was returning to me. Our stay was almost up. Black smoke was pouring out of the vessel's funnels. Papers and passengers had been inspected. Boris's official duty was done.

The whistle sounded.

As the steam shrieked into the air, there was a noise of hurried movement, a stumble, a woman's cry of anguish, and Hélène fell fainting on the deck. She had tripped over a coil of rope. The passengers thronged around her. I sprang to her side, Boris rushed to us, but the captain was cool.

"Call the surgeon!" he said sharply. "Better take the lady into my cabin."

A few moments after, the ship's doctor made his report. Hélène's ankle was badly sprained!

"How badly?" asked Boris, sharply. "She can be moved, I presume."

"It would cause her intense pain—perhaps permanent injury," replied the surgeon.

Then the captain and the young Russian lieutenant went into hasty consultation, the merchant officer at last breaking out: "But I must go on, commander! Think of my insurance, my ship, my cargo—I shall lose my place."

To this Boris replied anxiously: "Madame Lenox can't go on in this way. The colonel has no passport. It would never do!"

"I have a passport," I said "good to leave Russia *via* Eydtkuhnen, for myself and wife." I presented him the document on which our railroad tickets had been refused.

"Oh, yes; but this one is not good for Cronstadt. My orders are imperative!" said the young officer.

"But the sick lady!" said the surgeon, hurriedly.

"One moment!" cried Boris. Then he took me aside. "My dear Lenox, it is out of the ordinary routine to let any one leave Russia with passports marked from any other port or city, but I suppose in your case, if your wife is too ill to be taken off this boat, I might permit it, providing you give me your honor as a man to bring her back by the return steamer. Otherwise——"

"Otherwise?" said I.

His eyes met mine anxiously. "Otherwise the affair will be very serious for me. You as an army officer know what disobedience of orders means to a naval one," he replied.

I said: "I will see my wife, and tell you in a few moments whether she can be moved."

Then I went into the stateroom. Hélène was

lying on the lounge, her face apparently drawn by pain, her boot off, her ankle bandaged.

I saw the deftness with which she had conceived this plan. This affair had been arranged the night before. The Swedish captain was one of their order, and in league with her to get her out of Russia.

Her safety would give me safety. Oh, the temptation, the longing to accept it! But I knew it meant ruin to the brave young Russian sailor, my friend and relative, who paced the deck outside, impatiently. He would trust to my word of honor. She would leave the vessel at Stockholm; I could not detain her. It would be his destruction.

Then I closed the door, stepped to her, and whispered: "Get up! Put on your boot, and leave the ship with me!"

"I can't, Arthur! You are a barbarian, a fool too!" she whispered. "Don't you see this is life for both of us?"

"Yes," said I. "Life for us, but degradation and the Caucasus for him."

"That makes no difference! He is a Russian! Self-preservation! My Heaven, Arthur, you are not going to spoil our one chance for safety? Think of your wife! You will never see her again, if you do not help me now to escape!"

"No, no!" I gasped. "Don't tempt me!"

"Think of my love!" she cried; "for I will love you *now*, if you will spare me!" then burst out sobbing: "I dare not stay! I have been told the punishment that will be given! My God, I dare not! I am frightened! It was too awful to tell you! For God's sake, have pity!" and wrung her hands, for her nerves had given way to the prolonged strain and she was a picture of physical fear.

Then she broke out again: "Have mercy! Tell him you will take me to Stockholm and bring me back. Lie to him but *once,* for my sake!" Her tempting arms were around me, but it seemed to me that I almost despised her, as I thought of the gallant young sailor that she would sacrifice, whose career she would destroy, and whose life she would make one of horror and degradation—to save her miserable self.

"Get up!" I said sternly. "Put on your boot, or I will tell Boris Weletsky everything."

"And he?" she said.

"He will do his duty."

She rose up, looked me in the face, and saw I was immovable. Then she gave a great sigh, as of despair, and muttered: "You fool! you are going back to your destruction!" and growing calmer, whispered: "Very well! The comedy is ended! The tragedy begins! Tell Captain Boris that I am sufficiently recovered for you to carry me down to his boat;" then laughed hysterically, and astonished me with these words: "You have saved one brother, you have destroyed the other. But it is better that way. This naval gentleman is more worthy than the major of the *Garde.*"

I stepped out on deck and told Boris that on examination I found my wife had the fortitude to permit me to carry her down the gangway to his boat, rather than that he should be at any inconvenience or risk on our account.

I know by the sigh of relief he gave that it had taken a mighty weight from his mind.

Two minutes afterward, assisted by Boris, I carried Hélène to his boat, the Swedish captain and his doctor staring in astonishment after us.

In half an hour we were again in Cronstadt, and Hélène, partially recovered, leaning upon my arm, was assisted to a carriage. We were soon at the railroad depot, and an hour and a half afterward were in St. Petersburg, my wife looking at her watch very often. She was apparently in a feverish anxiety to reach our apartments.

"To the hotel, quick!" she cried. "I am very hungry; are you not, Arthur? I ordered dinner before we left, to be ready at six." Then she sighed: "I had hoped we would not be here to eat it. I might have lost all my trunks, and been very seasick

this evening; but now—*now,* there is but little between us and—" She pointed her thumb significantly at the great fortress over the river, with its
underground cells and mysterious horrors.

We entered our apartment, to find the table
already set and dinner waiting for us. I went into
my room, Hélène into hers; but while making my
toilet, as I was about to brush my hair, a little piece
of paper fell from the brush on the floor. I stooped
down and picked it up. It read:

"Be very careful of your wife this evening, I think Sacha
means to carry her off."

It was in the same handwriting as the note of
two days before — that of the French governess.
"Curse him! Even with death above me, Sacha should
never triumph!" I muttered to myself fiercely, and
strolled into the *salon.*

Linking this with Hélène's curious ruse on the
ship, I became suspicious. She would desert me
here and leave me alone a prey to Russian justice.

The dinner passed away. Nothing peculiar happened, though after the coffee I grew unusually
drowsy.

I fought against this. It overcame me. It seemed
to me as if the dinner I had eaten acted upon me
as my powders did. The room became hazy to me.

In it I saw the face of Sacha. I wanted to spring

up, seize him by the throat, to throttle him for daring to be here. I heard a faint murmur in the air, and a woman's voice—*her* voice—saying: "I have not given him too much—not as much as he gave me."

Then bliss came upon me and insensibility.

———

## CHAPTER XVI.

### THE LAST COUP OF THE DESPAIRING RAT.

IT was morning.

Some one touched me on the shoulder and said: "Pardon me; I have a message from Baron Friedrich."

I saw a gentleman in plain clothes standing by my bedside.

I knew it had come. The hand that had been hovering over me so long had fallen. I was in the grasp of Russian justice. The man said politely: "I would not have awakened you, but my orders were imperative and immediate, Colonel Lenox. Would you be kind enough to dress yourself and come with me? I hope the business will be short enough to permit your return for breakfast."

As I stepped out of bed and made my morning toilet I knew that I would breakfast no more in that hotel. The chill was on my heart—that shivering coldness that comes to those who have before them nothing but despair.

As soon as I was ready, this gentleman requested

me to follow him. Together we passed through the *salon*. There I saw two other men in plain clothes, but with alert demeanor, seated quietly, apparently waiting orders.

I had expected to find Hélène there before me, perhaps with manacles upon her fair wrists—perchance with a gag in her pretty mouth; but she was not visible.

However, I knew she was as surely in their hands as I was, as I heard her breathing, deep and strong, coming over the transom, and knew when she awoke it would be in the clutches of Russian justice.

I was about to speak to her when the gentleman at my side said: "Pardon me; you must come with me at once, without word to madame. These are my orders."

So I followed him down to a carriage which was waiting in the courtyard of the hotel, and together we drove up the Nevsky to the local police station —the one devoted to the more immediate affairs of Russian Justice. Here, passing through guards, who opened for my companion, I stepped upstairs and was shown into a comfortable office. Two doors, besides the one I had entered, opened into the apartment. Here Baron Friedrich was seated at his desk, a couple of *gendarmes* in attendance.

Dismissing these, he sprang up and said: "My dear colonel, you will pardon my troubling you before breakfast, but this was a matter of moment. We can, however, I hope, settle the affair in a very few minutes. Permit me to offer you a cigar."

Attempting nonchalance, I accepted it, and tried to smoke, but I did not enjoy it. Noting this, he laughed slightly and remarked: "It is not quite so good as those we had on the road from Wilna, a week ago. But to come to the point at once, as I presume you are in a hurry for your breakfast. The police have apprehended a lady travelling in Russia under a passport which states that she is your wife. Now of course we know your wife is with you at the De l'Europe; consequently this impostor has been brought here simply that you may say she is not your wife, and then we will deal with her as one who travels under false papers."

These words, so kindly in appearance, so awful in import, agitated, horrified me. My heart got into my mouth.

My suspense did not last long.

"She will be here in a moment," said the baron, "and it will require but two words from you." He touched a bell, and to the answering attendant said: "You may bring the lady in—the one in waiting."

A moment after the door opened, and in pretty travelling dress, but agitated and indignant, a lady entered, threw off her veil, and cried: "What new outrage is this?" then shrieked: "Arthur! thank God, you're alive! I feared, from the telegram, you were dead." And my *true* wife—my blue-eyed one from Paris—had thrown herself, sobbing, into my arms, and with tears, caresses, and endearing words, and pantings of joy, had nearly broken my wicked heart at the thought that for seven days I had forgotten her for the glances of another.

On this scene the baron looked, a smile of supreme happiness and triumph shining through his blue spectacles, though I noted he knocked the ashes of his cigar off nervously. Then he said suddenly: "Colonel Lenox, who is this woman?"

"My wife, my true wife!" I cried. "My God! you did not suppose that I would deny her and leave her to the tender mercies of Russian justice?"

"Russian justice!" cried Laura, my wife. "Russian justice is an outrage. I don't care"—for I had put up my hand warningly—"I *will* speak. I received your telegram saying that you were dangerously ill here, and asking me to come and nurse you. Your letter had told me of the epidemic raging here. I took the train from Paris for St. Petersburg at once, using the passport I had from the American minister, and 'viséed' by the Russian ambassador to France. Immediately after crossing the frontier I was arrested and brought here under surveillance, kept here this morning as a criminal. Now come with me and demand justice from those in authority above this wicked little fat man. Let us go to the American Legation at once!"

At this I gave a hoarse, horrible laugh of despair, and Baron Friedrich said: "Pardon me; I must part your husband from you, madame, though *you* will be shortly free."

"And my husband!" she cried. "What of him?"

The baron's blue eyeglasses were impenetrable. "That *afterward*," he said significantly. "At present, madame, I offer you my humble apologies for the arrest you have been subject to and the misapprehension that has caused it, but—" He made a sign.

I gave her one last, despairing kiss; she was led back from me into the apartment from which she had come; the door closed on her. My God! would I ever see her again in this life?

As I thought of my many sins, both of omission and commission, in my military career, I feared never in the other.

"Now," cried Baron Friedrich, his manner losing that of friendship and becoming that of the Minister of Justice, "your explanation of this, sir. Your con-

fession! Reserve is useless, for now I know who your
other wife is, and I have HER!"

There was triumph and gloating in his eyes as
he spoke, and his fat little body seemed to expand
and become larger and more potent. He touched a
bell, and gave some hurried orders to the person
that came in to him. What these were I don't know;
I was thinking of myself. Then he turned to me and
said, as judge addresses criminal: "Now, sir!"

All reserve was useless. I hurriedly began to tell
him the story of my adventure, from the frontier on.
He occasionally interrupted me, tapping upon the
desk and saying: "Good! that is right. Now I know
I have her! I have her!! She is mine!!!" as a man
would shout at a bauble that he has longed for all
his life, something unattainable, something he could
never hope for, but has now, to his astonishment and
happiness, in his hands.

While I was in the midst of this, in fact, before
I had given him the details of our arrival in St.
Petersburg, there was a rap on the door.

"One moment," said Baron Friedrich; then cried
"Come in!"

An under official stepped to him and said: "The
Councillor Constantine Weletsky desires to see you;"
and looking upon me, whispered: "It is upon his
business, I think."

"Very well, admit him."

A second after, my noble Russian relative entered the apartment hastily, wildness in his eye and humiliation and sorrow in his bearing, and before either Friedrich or I could say a word, burst out upon us:

"I know, my poor Lenox, the business that has brought you here—the awful misery that has come upon you through one of my house, though I disown him and curse him for his outrage upon the rights of hospitality!"

"Of whom are you talking?" cried Friedrich, hastily.

"Of my nephew, Sacha Weletsky, major of the *Chevalier Garde,* whose commission I shall beg the czar as a personal favor to cancel, for he has degraded Russian manhood and my family by eloping with the wife of my guest." And the old gentleman wiped tears of rage and anguish from his eyes as both Friedrich and I gazed at each other amazed.

Then he broke out again:

"My dear Lenox, I begged you to bring your wife to my house to live! Why did you not accept my hospitality? Could you not see that I wished the shield of my own roof-tree to be put over your wife to keep her from the attentions, the arts, the intrigues of my scoundrelly nephew, who respects neither relationship nor hospitality?"

"My dear councillor," interrupted Baron Friedrich, "what strange tale are you telling us?"

"I am telling you the *truth!* I have discovered this morning that last evening my nephew Alexander Weletsky eloped and departed from Russia with the wife of this gentleman here, my guest, my relative."

"Impossible!" cried Baron Friedrich, while I burst out into a hideous laugh.

This was echoed by the head of police, though I could see that for the moment he grew pale. Then he said pointedly: "I have one upon her track for the last twenty-four hours from whom she could never escape. The lady whom you say has eloped with your nephew, my dear Weletsky, will be here in five minutes to show you you are mistaken."

But even as he spoke the door was thrown open, and Baron Friedrich grew pale, then reeled and clutched his desk convulsively, while both Constantine and I gave a gasp of astonishment; for into our presence, bound and gagged, was brought, not the figure of the graceful Hélène, but the lithe form of the French governess, Mademoiselle Eugénie de Launay, whose dark eyes were flashing fire, and whose lips, if they could have spoken, would have cried out in rage and anger.

"What have we here?" gasped Constantine.

"Ungag that woman instantly," commanded Friedrich. Then he said, hurriedly but politely: "And may I ask you to withdraw for a few minutes, Councillor Weletsky?"

I was about to follow my relative, when Friedrich's little fat hand fell on my shoulder. "As for you, remain here," he whispered; "YOU ARE MINE!" And my heart grew chilly, though I looked with astonishment at the interview that now took place.

The moment she was released the De Launay was about to give tongue, when Friedrich stopped her, and said: "Silence! Answer my questions. Not another word. Where is the woman who has been travelling under the passport as this man's wife?" and pointed to me.

"She has fled."

"Fled! My God! When? Where?"

"With Sacha Weletsky, last night."

"At what hour?"

"Seven o'clock."

"Where to?"

"I do not know."

"One moment; she could not have got out of reach so soon; that is impossible." Then he commenced to wring his hands and groan. "My God, *if* she has escaped!" Next cried: "A telegraph clerk, quick! She could never have escaped by this time. Eydtkuhnen?—the distance is too great. Cronstadt? —guarded. There is only one other place in these few hours by which she could have left Russia— Wiborg!" He rang his bell, and directed: "Telegraph Wiborg instantly. Ask if any ship left there last night. If so, what passengers. Telegraph particularly if Sacha Weletsky, major in the *Chevalier Garde* has been seen there. Was there a woman in his company?—if so, under what passport she travelled. If there now, arrest them at once." Then he said suddenly: "Telegraph their descriptions to all railroad stations within one thousand versts of St. Petersburg, and order their arrest." Then he paced the floor talking to himself aloud: "They would not have dared to hide themselves in the country? No. Sacha knows too much for that; that means delayed but certain, ultimate arrest." He turned again to the woman, and said: "Tell me the details. I had supposed you *sure,* because I knew you *hated* the woman you were watching."

"Yes," cried I, wildly, "but *loved* the man!"

"What, loved Sacha Weletsky! My God! is that the clew to your conduct?" he cried. "Answer me!"

The woman fell down before him, wringing her hands and sobbing: "Have mercy!"

"Answer me—the truth! That is the only way to get mercy from Baron Friedrich. The *truth!"*

"I had your instructions. I went there to watch! My God! do you suppose that I would have permitted the man I loved to run away with the woman I hated if I could have stopped it? I was on watch at the hotel all day. I saw this gentleman and her go to Cronstadt."

"Did she hope to escape me there?" cried Friedrich, in a voice that showed me Hélène's plan on the *Dalecarlia* would have surely failed.

"Then, at half-past five, I saw them return to their rooms, where the waiters had already arranged dinner for them.

"Twenty minutes after Sacha entered their apartments, and I watched more eagerly. In ten minutes more he came out again, and I spoke to him, to reproach him for his perfidy to me, for I loved him."

"And he beguiled you?" sneered Friedrich, in an awful voice.

"Y-e-s, he—he——"

"*What?*"

"He said: 'Eugénie, you are jealous of a grandmamma. You foolish child; I don't love antiques.' He spoke to me in the tones I adore and could not resist; he whispered: 'Wait here for me a moment; I will prove to you I am not going to run away, by spending the next three hours with you.' A moment after he said: 'You look tired; Lenox and his wife are in the next room, I will bring you a cup of coffee from their dinner-table.' He brought it to me with loving words, and I drank it——"

"And then?" whispered Baron Friedrich, hoarsely.

"Then he talked to me a little more, and I grew sleepy, and I felt his arms leading me into the room; and this morning I was gagged as I awoke in my rival's bed, and brought here."

"And your cursed passion for that Russian jacka-napes has destroyed the *coup* of my life. Don't expect mercy from me!" cried Friedrich, for Eugénie was fawning upon him.

But just here the telegraph clerk entered hurriedly, and placed a despatch in front of Baron Friedrich, at which he uttered a growl of rage. His face grew pale, his hands clutched themselves together, as if grasping something that was intangible and had slipped through his fingers. He said: "Remove that woman! Leave me alone with the American!"

Then he muttered as we faced each other: "This telegram says the woman I had thought my own has escaped me. That Major Sacha Weletsky travelled to Wiborg, an outpost of St. Petersburg—no passport being needed, as officer of the day of his regiment. That he demanded permission as an officer of the czar, on the personal business of the emperor, to leave by the steamer sailing last night for Denmark. With him a woman, presenting passport of Eugénie de Launay, special agent of secret detective bureau of the Russian Government—general passport, permitting travel anywhere in pursuit of her duties. This vessel steamed out at half-past eleven last night. It is impossible for me to overtake her. She has passed Cronstadt, even Rewel, by this time. She is upon the high seas, and safe from me for the time being."

Then he looked upon me as the buzzard looks upon his carrion. "But *you* are mine!" he said, with a little chuckle. "You who have brought her into Russia, have introduced her to your relatives, even conducted her into the presence of the czar, under a false passport, as your legal spouse. You are mine!—*all mine!*—IN MY RAT-TRAP!" And he gloated over me.

But here the inspiration of my life came to me— the happy thought, born of despair, for which I pat myself on my shoulder every day of my life that it saved! This came to me, and I gave him the last *coup* of the despairing rat.

I cried: "No; I am as safe as you are! Listen to me for your own salvation, my dear friend, Baron Friedrich. True, I admitted this lady under my passport. I have violated enough Russian law for you to send me to Siberia."

"Perhaps do more," said the baron, dryly.

"But you cannot do this without inquiry. I am a well-known American citizen. I am not a person you can intern quietly, without one word being said.

Inquiry must be made by my legation. You can set up the facts of my case, you can punish me, doubtless; my country will not interfere in such a matter. I know that. But dare you tell the facts to the czar, your master? Dare you let him know that you let his arch-enemy into Russia—that you spoke to her, you kissed her hand, and did *not know her?* That you let her into his presence so that she would have murdered him?"

"Murdered him!" This was a gasp from Friedrich.

*"Murdered him!"* I felt confident now I was winning, and my tone grew stronger.

He said: "Hush! not so loud!"

"Dare you let the czar know that it was *my* hand, not *yours,* that saved him from death by her pistol?"

"Impossible!" he cried. "What are you telling me?"

"What I will prove to you. Listen to me for your official salvation!" Then I told him everything. How the opium drug in my hands had saved the czar from the hunter that had him in sight and marked down as quarry.

He did not answer me, but pressed his hands over his eyes, as if thinking deeply.

"Now," I said, "you told me once it was *their*

heads or *yours!* Dare you tell your master that she has escaped from your hands—this woman who is his terror as well as yours? Your best chance of safety is my safety—which is SILENCE! Get my wife and me outside of Russia at once. Let us see no one. I don't mind if you send me to the frontier guarded. And, above all, don't let my wife loose in society here, because then they will know there was a false one by my side for a week."

Here Friedrich gave a hideous chuckle and cried: "And your wife will know there was a false husband here for a week. Ha—ah! Lenox! I will turn you over to your wife's vengeance; that will be greater than the czar's."

I gave an answering chuckle also to this, for I knew it meant safety to me. I said: "Yes, put us together, confine us in a car, but ship us out of Russia."

"At once!" he said. Then his old friendship for me seemed to return, and he cried: "When I go to Paris we will have a pleasant time together."

"Yes, if you say nothing to my wife," said I.

A moment after he remarked: "You had better not return to the hotel."

"But," said I, "breakfast——"

"Take it with me. Your wife has been already provided for." He rang his bell, ordered breakfast for us both in his office, then directed my luggage brought from the De l'Europe to me, and remarked maliciously: "I presume I had better have the lady's trunks forwarded to your Paris address."

At which suggestion I nearly fainted.

"You would like to see that noble old Russian, Constantine, and bid him good-by?" he remarked.

"No," I muttered.

"Ah! the shame of injured hospitality is on your head, not his," he said; then broke out: "Oh, why did you not tell me when you lunched with me? My heavens! what a prize she would have been! For me, honor and power; for you, half a million roubles!"

I told him I was too frightened.

"Frightened? Faugh! you loved her," he jeered; then said seriously: "When a beautiful woman is the criminal, she has all the passions of men to make them shield her from us. Because she was lovely you risked death, and Sacha, that miserable, has ruined himself forever."

"But you didn't suspect her then?" I said.

"No; I thought her appearance very young for a grandmother, but had seen such things before. Your reception by the Weletskys brushed that away. Oh, she was deep in her wisdom, astute in her devices. She forgot herself but *once*. When the music of the mazurka got into her heart, her blood answered it, and she danced as none but a Pole, Hungarian, or Russian could have done. No Miss Vanderbilt-Astor could have danced the national dance as she did. *Then* I suspected; but your introductions were so good. Weletsky stands so high with the czar I dared not make a mistake, and so I telegraphed Paris and sent your *true* wife a message that you were ill—and my little ruse was successful. By the. bye, madame is awaiting you impatiently."

Two hours after, as the one o'clock train dashed out of the Warsaw railway station, my wife and I left St. Petersburg under surveillance of the police, with orders to speak to no one; but I travelled very pleasantly, for I was as happy as a man who had escaped from the jaws of death, and listened to my wife's anathemas on the Russian police, who were treating her as a nihilist and a criminal, she claimed, and her threats that she would never let me visit Russia again, with complacence, even rapture.

All this journey Baron Friedrich was on the train with us; in fact, he went with us to the frontier. At Eydtkuhnen he bade me good-by. He said: "Lenox, Russia is not the proper country for you."

"I agree with you," remarked I.

"You are a peculiar man," said he. "I would

offer you a great deal to join our forces, to come under my orders."

"No, thank you," laughed I.

"Ah!" said he, tapping me on the shoulder, "you are an infernal idiot, with some flashes of genius, that's what you are, my dear Lenox. Adieu!"

———

## CHAPTER XVII.

### AT THE OPERA IN PARIS.

SOME three months after this, in the height of the season, my wife and I, rather late in the evening, stepped out of our carriage at the portals of the Grand Opera, in Paris.

It was a snowy night. The electric lights flashed upon the gorgeous equipages of the rich—the rags of the poor. As I assisted my Laura from the carriage, and was leading her into the grand entrance, a hand was placed upon my arm, a voice came to my ear that made me start; a voice I had not heard for three months. I turned around and beheld Sacha! His coat was a little shiny. He was no more the dashing swell of the *Chevalier Garde;* no more the high roller of the Imperial Yacht Club.

He whispered: "For God's sake, I want to see you, Lenox!"

"Very well," said I. "As soon as I have taken madame to her box, I will speak to you."

"Aha!" he said, a curious significance in his voice, "you have consoled yourself quickly!"

"Hush!" I muttered; "I will see you in a few moments." And taking my wife, who had looked rather astonished at my interview with a man who appeared to her part beggar, part tramp, part *chevalier d'industrie,* went with my Laura to our box, and made her comfortable.

Then I said: "You must excuse me for a few moments."

"And why?"

"A gentleman downstairs——"

"Gentleman?"

"Well—man—wishes to see me."

"Case of charity?"

"Yes," I said, "partially so; I think he wants me to get him a position."

Then I went down, feeling very uncomfortable. If this wretched, reckless fellow, whose commission I learned had been cancelled in the *Garde,* who had been expelled from the Imperial Yacht Club, whose property had been confiscated for his escapade, knew the *whole* truth, what a power he had over me. If he whispered it to Laura—good heavens!

As I joined him he remarked: "You do not wish to see me?"

"No," I said; "why should I?"

"But I wish to see you."

"Come this way," I said, and led him into a neighboring *café* where we might have both quiet and privacy. I offered him a drink. He took it. "Now," said I, shortly, "what do you want?"

"My God! have you not heard how I have been treated? I have been cashiered, my estates confiscated, my name erased from the roll of Russian nobility. I have nothing left. That she-devil has deprived me of everything but you—my dear Lenox—but you!"

"What do you want?" I repeated hoarsely.

"I want assistance. I know now she was not your wife. Yet how she played me! She accepted my escort; she lured me to fly with her, from you, as I thought; but it was really from Russian justice, and *ruined me!* And what recompense did she give me? Nothing! *nothing!* NOTHING! Not even a kiss! As soon as on the high seas she claimed the protection of the Danish captain of the steamer, and laughed in my face, and said she hated me and all Russians, and loved to ruin them as she had ruined me; and that you had been her plaything as well as I. Aha! my dear Lenox, we know each other, we appreciate each other. You understand! I am a man of honor. I would not betray you to your wife. No, I do not wish to do that, because, though ruined in money matters, I am still a man of honor!"

"Though you would have robbed me of my wife. You thought she was my wife when you eloped with her."

"Ah! that is the way of the world. Every man for himself, with the ladies, my dear Lenox."

"What do you wish me to do?" I asked.

"This—simply give me a chance, an opportunity. I have been cleaned out of my last rouble at Monte Carlo. Lend me two hundred and fifty dollars, that I may go to America. It is a haven for the unfortunate. There I have youth, strength, and perhaps not altogether a lack of *finesse* and ability, and am still a man of honor."

Though still a man of honor, I thought it safer for my married happiness that he should have no chance to make any embarrassing disclosure to my wife.

"Very well!" said I. "To-morrow morning I will meet you here and give you the money." Which I did, and he has since departed for America, where I hear he is now the enterprising manager of a Parisian opera troupe, and flirts with his *prime-donne* with as much recklessness as he did with the beauties of St. Petersburg.

Then I returned to my wife and sat beside her, glad that she was so interested in the music and the sight of a beautiful woman in a box opposite, upon whom she had put her opera-glass, that she did not ask any questions.

A moment after she handed me her lorgnette,

and said: "Arthur, look across—the third box from the stage—and tell me if that lady is not one of the most beautiful you have ever seen in your life."

I used my opera-glass as requested. It nearly dropped from my hands upon the heads of those below us. The lady whose face I gazed upon was Hélène, more beautiful, radiant, charming, alluring than ever!

"You know something about her," said my wife, perhaps a little suspiciously. "I noted your start."

"Ah!" said I, "she was the lady that you were supposed to be. The Russian police in St. Petersburg arrested *you* in mistake for *her.*"

"Oh! what a compliment! She is so lovely!" said my wife. "Let me look at her again. Ahem, Arthur, am I as beautiful as that woman?"

I said with the diplomacy born of twenty years of matrimony: "In my eyes, my dear."

"You know something about her? Tell me."

Then I related to her the intrigues of this fair Nihilist conspirator. How I had heard that ambassadors had been compromised by her; that she was always working for one cause—her own revenge and the freedom of her country. I told my wife everything that I knew about Hélène, except that for seven days in Russia she had been my official wife. This, with the reserve born of matrimony, is still my secret, though I have fears it will not always be.

Thinking boldness was safety, I said: "You know I met the lady in St. Petersburg. If you do not mind I will step over and_say a word to her."

"Certainly; tell me what she says. I am anxious to hear more of her."

Then I walked round to the box, and in answer to my knock was told to enter. Hélène was there, a Turkish attaché bowing over her, a couple of Austrian officers of high rank seated near her, a young American millionaire looking love into her eyes.

She started slightly as I entered, then said: "I had been expecting you, Colonel Lenox. I saw you across the theatre. The lady with you is your wife, is she not?"

"Yes," replied I, striving to fight down a tenderness in my voice, "but not my official wife."

"Official wife! What new wrinkle in matrimony is that?" asked the American.

"That," said Hélène, with a little smile, "is our secret."

Just then she started, trembled, and looked at me. I turned pale also. The strains of the last act of "Un ballo" were beginning—that same immortal dance music that has murder in it, that same floating melody that had surrounded us when she fell fainting into my arms as she grasped for the pistol to slay the Autocrat of all the Russias.

I stepped out of the box and wondered how many more men's lives and loves she would risk or sacrifice for her revenge—her patriotism. What would become of "My Official Wife"?

THE END.

PRINTING OFFICE OF THE PUBLISHER.

www.ingramcontent.com/pod-product-compliance
Lightning Source LLC
Chambersburg PA
CBHW060610030726
47498CB00005B/1618